# FORTUNE HAUNTER

HAUNTED EVERLY AFTER MYSTERIES
BOOK FIVE

REGINA WELLING
ERIN LYNN

Willow Hill
BOOKS

# CONTENTS

# FORTUNE HAUNTER

I managed to go six whole months without stumbling over a dead body—a personal record for me. A record that shattered like delicate crystal on a fine summer morning. Don't laugh; you probably have your own hurdles in life, and I hope they have nothing to do with the dearly departed.

Unfortunately, mine do.

And that was why my dog, Molly, dropped to her haunches and whined. The sight of a pair of skinny legs sprawled across the rocky trail at the bottom of the slate quarry didn't surprise me as much as it should have done. I knew those legs by the three-inch cuffs and frayed material. Only one man in town wore flannel-lined jeans even in the burgeoning heat of early June.

"That's Delly Harper," I said, and from what I could see, old Delly wasn't moving. My hand flew up to cover my mouth as I rushed forward to call out, "Are you all right?"

Utter silence but for the distant sound of running water told its own tale.

Not too far from where we stood, a bend of the Mooselick River brought it close to the long-defunct Barrow quarry where Drew had brought me to face my fears after nearly dying there almost a year before. Neither of us expected to find anything other than my lost courage.

"Do you see him?" Distracted, I let go of Molly's leash and clamped my hand on Drew's arm. "He's not moving. I think he's dead."

Of course, he was dead. How could he be anything but dead with his eyes all glazed over and staring directly into the emerging sun? He had to be dead, or else he'd have blinked by now—probably not the most astute of observations, but it's amazing the random thoughts that pop into one's mind during moments of great stress.

Too late, Drew spun me away. "You don't have to look."

"Can't unsee him now." The sight was already burned into my corneas. With shaking hands, I pulled out my cell and checked to see if I had a signal. One bar. Not enough. And wouldn't you know, the only spot in the belly of the pit that had more than two bars was almost on top of the corpse—just my luck.

But even with my feet planted far enough away and leaning over the body, the connection refused to go through the first time. While I waited, I got an uncomfortably close look at the awkward way Delly's head no longer lined up with his body.

"Broken neck," Drew stated the obvious. "Looks like he fell."

My mind helpfully supplied an imaginary movie of Delly sliding over the edge, his arms pinwheeling as he tried to keep his balance. I even heard the faint echo of a startled cry.

A shudder shook me as I tapped 9-1-1 into my phone again. "How sad to die out here alone."

Just saying the word alone sent my guts into knots, but I dismissed the fluttering sensation and waited for the phone to ring on the other end of the line. Finally, it did.

Whether or not the dread settling in the pit of my stomach came from a sixth sense or just from close proximity to yet one more dead body, I couldn't tell. It wasn't my first time, so I knew better than to disturb anything as I leaned over the body and listened to the phone ringing.

My least favorite dispatcher picked up on the second ring. "What's your emergency?"

"Hey, Carol Ann. I…uh…need to report an accident."

"Ernie," she shrieked loud enough I had to yank my phone away from my ear. "It's that Everly Dupree on the line. Says she needs to report an accident. Probably killed someone again."

"What do you mean *again*?" I heard disdain in her voice and the sucking sound of her straw draining something out of a plastic cup. "Just put Ernie on, okay?"

The next thing I heard was the terse voice of our town lawman. "Polk."

"I did not kill anyone."

A sigh. "You never do, and yet someone's always dead. Who is it this time?"

"Molly," I shouted when Molly's head went up, and she raced out of sight in a blur of sleek chocolate fur and pounding feet.

"Molly who? Have you gone mad?" I could all but hear Ernie yank the phone away from his ear.

I didn't waste time arguing the point. "Sorry, my dog just took off. It's Delly Harper. We found him in the quarry." I pictured our location on a map in my head. "Near where the river bends in toward the pit. Behind the Jackson place."

Ernie and I might not see eye-to-eye on everything, but there were two things I knew about him. One, a little judicious flirting might get a girl out of a ticket, but he was a good cop even when it cost him dearly. And two, he didn't—as a rule—spout profanity on the job. Until today, anyway, but I sensed true grief behind the spate of cussing.

"I told that half-witted fool to put a fence along the edge of that cliff." He swore some more. "Probably got himself half-snockered on cheap wine, went digging for those stupid jars again, and lost his footing."

"Maybe. I'm not getting any closer than I have to, but I don't smell booze on him from here." I went on to describe the condition and approximate location of the body, but the quarry pit wound a fair way and looked very different from below than from above.

One path through rocks and bushes looks a lot like any other, and while I had a general idea where we were, I couldn't give exact directions.

"I'll have Drew hike back out to the main road and wait for you. He can show you the way."

Given a choice between dealing with the dog while keeping an eye on the body and getting turned around on a path I hadn't paid enough attention to on the way in seemed like a no-brainer to me.

"Don't touch anything. I'll be there in ten, fifteen at the most." The line clicked dead.

"Like I didn't know that already." At least this time, the death looked to be from natural causes. Still, once the call ended, I put some distance between myself and the body just in case Delly's spirit hadn't gone yet.

"Your hands are shaking," Drew took them in his, stilled most of the trembling with his touch. A deep breath took care of the rest and let me center myself again.

After my marriage ended in a bitter divorce, I hadn't planned on dating anyone. Not ever. Once burned and all that jazz. I hadn't counted on meeting Drew Parker when he opened up a gym in Mooselick River, and it wasn't only his body that sparked a powerful attraction between us right from the first moment.

Drew carries an ineffable air of calm and reassurance—and yes, I realize I've just made him sound boring, but he's not. He's the perfect blend of confident but not cocky. Hot, but not conceited. And if attraction had been all I felt, I could have resisted falling into a relationship. I've worked hard at not being the type of woman to be led around by her hormones.

But there was more to it, to him and to us, than that. It's hard to describe, but being with him made me feel both protected and more resilient—and not only because of the self-protection skills he'd taught me. This morning's quarry hike had been Drew's idea. He thought it would empower me if I faced the fear brought on by nearly dying here. It was the first step, he said, toward us eventually rappelling down the face of the quarry in tandem.

That would not be happening, but he still held out hope. I like that about him.

From not too far away, I heard a short bark and then the unmistakable sound of my dog's paws pounding the ground in the opposite direction she'd left from. One of my favorite things about Molly is that she runs as she does everything else—with great abandon but absolutely no sense of style or grace.

"See, here comes Molly back again. I think we should wait for her and then you can come with me. There's nothing more to do for Delly, and it's not like he's going anywhere."

A sharp chill that had nothing to do with the damp morning crept over the small clearing and over me. When Drew didn't so much as bat an eyelash, my heart sank. Dead body, creepy chill in the air—all signs pointed to one thing: ghost

And that was why, when Delly shivered into sight behind Drew, I wasn't even a little bit surprised.

Accidental death?

Probably not. Every ghost I'd met so far had been the victim of either out-and-out murder or, in one case, unsolved vehicular manslaughter. I could get lucky and find out Delly had some other type of unfinished business that kept him on the wrong side of the veil, but I wouldn't bet the farm on it.

"No." I sighed, shrugged the backpack straps off my shoulders, and settled down on a flat rock away from the body. "He's not, but it doesn't seem right to just leave him here alone. You go, Molly will stay with me. I'm okay now, and we'll be fine. The faster Ernie gets here, the sooner we can go home."

Delly paced the few steps between his body and the trail, his gaze darting left then right before he locked eyes with me. He picked up on my subtle head-shake, and though he quivered like a nervous chihuahua with the effort, kept silent.

"Go," I repeated. "You'll move faster alone."

"Okay, but stay right here. Don't go off on your own. Take this." Drew pulled a leather-sheathed knife from the side pocket of his hiking shorts. "Just in case."

In case of what, I wondered as he kissed me.

I noted the crestfallen look on Drew's face. "I'm sorry we won't get to finish our empowerment exercise."

Not many men I'd known would have heard a woman utter that phrase without rolling their eyes, but Drew had used it first.

"It's okay. Another time." He kissed me again, then before I could do more than frown at the false note I heard in his tone, he headed back the way we had come, leaving me temporarily alone with Delmar Harper.

Panting with her efforts, Molly arrived before

Drew's backpack disappeared from sight. She danced up to me, dropped a piece of moldering red cloth at my feet, and went into a crouch with her hind end up in the air—her *waiting for me to throw the ball* pose.

While I eyed the filthy remains of what I thought might once have been part of the bodice of a dress, Delly spoke.

"She's gonna die if you don't save her." He looked at me with eyes round as saucers. "Promise me you won't let Pearl die."

Without thinking too much about it, I tucked the scrap of cloth in the side pocket of my backpack to show Molly this wasn't playtime. She gave me the doggy equivalent of a dirty look, then settled down to wait in case I changed my mind.

"Who's Pearl? Was she with you when you...um?" For all I knew, Delly didn't realize he was dead. I've heard that happens sometimes. "Where is she? What does she look like?" I launched off the rock and prepared to run in whatever direction he indicated.

My heart bumped a bit in my chest at the thought of this Pearl in mortal danger. All Drew's warnings drifted away on a rush of adrenaline. I had to go help; it was a moral imperative.

"She's white." I hadn't thought his eyes could bug

out any more than they usually did, but Delly proved me wrong. Already on the high side for a man, his voice rose to nearly a squeak, and I thought he'd chosen an odd way to begin describing someone. "Green eyes, long hair, and a dark patch behind her left ear."

I'd grown up in Mooselick River and figured that since I'd moved back, I'd met all or most of the newer residents between one town event or another. Still, I couldn't remember anyone who looked like that.

Blame my stupidity on the adrenaline rush, but I didn't put two and two together until he said, "Pearl's my cat. You have to take care of her now that I'm gone."

Once he said *cat*, I remembered having run into him in the pet food aisle of the grocery store one time and tuning him out as he told me about her.

My pause to dredge up the memory must have freaked him out. "Promise me you won't let her die."

Along with the higher pitch to his tone, Delly's otherworldly energy kicked up a notch until I felt the hum of it in the back of my throat.

"I promise," I said. Anything to stop the rising tension. "Give me the name of whichever family member she should go to, and I'll make the arrangements for you, okay?" I thought he'd relax a little with that fear put to rest, but he didn't, so I tried to reassure him. "Now that we have Pearl all settled, you should see a bright light. Just go into the light, and you'll find your rest."

Hope crept in and settled somewhere around the area of my chest when Delly looked around for the light. Hope went up in flames, burned to ash, and drifted away on the bitter wind of disappointment when his gaze came back to my face.

"But I don't have any real family left." His Adam's apple twitched. "You have to take her. Say you will."

It probably wasn't an adrenaline hangover that set my head banging like a drum.

Then I thought of something. "I have a dog. See her right there? She's a big girl, and hasn't ever met a cat. I bet Pearl would be terrified at the sight of her."

"Pshaw," Delly dismissed the notion. "Pearl don't take crap from anyone or anything. Ain't a dog in the world could back my girl down."

None of this was getting me any closer to finding out what had happened in the unfortunate man's final hours, so I gave in. "Okay. Tell me where you lived, and I'll swing by and pick her up on my way home." What was one more inherited pet?

"Right up there," Delly pointed to the cliff above. "Everyone calls it the Jackson place, but it's been mine for the last twenty years."

"Now, about that light. Do you see it?"

"Naw, don't see no light." Because that would have been too easy.

I sighed. "Okay. Can you tell me what you were doing out here?"

Still pacing, Delly told his story.

"Everybody knows Clint Jackson panned gold along this here part of the river for over thirty years. I happen to know he found himself a fair bit, too."

I'd heard the legend of Clint's folly from my father, who'd never put much credence into the notion there'd ever been more than a few gold flakes in any body of water in this part of the state. Still, according to those who did buy into the story, Clint Jackson had hit pay dirt in the bend of the river near where he'd built his house. The same bend that dipped along behind the quarry.

"Old Clint, he didn't trust no assayer to give him a fair price, and he didn't believe in banks, so he sealed up his gold in glass jars and buried them on his property." A hank of dirty blond hair fluttered as

Delly nodded like his neck was made of spring. "There's seven of them in the ground."

Knowing I'd regret asking, I did it anyway. "How could you possibly know that?" Some of the details filtered in from the far reaches of my memory. "Didn't Clint die in like—" I did some quick math in my head. "—the seventies or something?"

I looked at Delly's tall, lined forehead, his features all scrunched together at the bottom of his face—the ghost version because I wanted to avoid looking at the real one—and tried to figure out if he and Clint could have been friends.

My chances of getting hired at the circus for guessing ages and weights were right up there with my chances of curing cancer, but to me, Delly didn't look old enough to fit the math.

Head bobbing, he said, "He came down with the sugar, Uncle Clint did. Didn't hold no truck with doctors, neither. Stubbed his toe on a rock, and the sore festered, but Clint didn't tell no one until his foot was half-rotted off. Gangrene took him right in his own bed with my daddy sitting vigil. I think I was eleven years old at the time."

He'd said Uncle Clint, so that solved some of the mystery.

A sad story, to be sure, but I needed him to speed up the telling, so I circled my hand in the gesture to hurry it up. A gesture he either didn't understand or chose to ignore because he only went into more detail about how his uncle's property had come down to him while the time ticked past.

"Right before the end, Clint told my daddy where to find the gold, 'cept he told it in a sort of code. Else he wasn't quite right in his mind because I ain't never found a single jar, and I been looking for it all my life, just like my daddy did. Cost me dear, though, when I had to choose between the old farm and what my daddy left me. Always figured I'd strike it rich and have them both. I guess that didn't pan out too well."

"And that's what you were doing when you… when it happened?" I gestured vaguely toward the body. "Were you alone?"

"First rule of treasure hunting, you don't do it as a group 'less you plan on sharing the booty, and I didn't." Delly pursed his lips. Out of respect for his being dead and all, I managed not to laugh at his expression but pushed a little harder when I heard the faint wail of approaching sirens in the distance.

"So, you didn't talk to or see anyone before you fell?"

Delly took a moment to think, then his eyes rounded, and he began to speak.

"Oh, I did see—" And he poofed. Standard operating procedure when a ghost tries to talk about their own murder. At least he wouldn't be yammering in my ear when Ernie showed up. Sometimes it's the small things that make life—or death—easier.

# CHAPTER TWO

"I'd like to stick around if you don't mind. My dad was friends with him," I said when Drew suggested our presence was no longer necessary to the process of bagging and tagging the body. "I feel like it's the least I can do, and someone has to take his cat."

Ernie muttered something unintelligible except for the word nosy. I ignored Drew's furrowed brow and let both men think what they wanted.

"How do you know he has a cat?" Drew wondered. "Had a cat, I mean."

"He told me once in the grocery store." Not a lie.

"Do you mind?" Ernie interrupted. "We're trying to work here."

About halfway through the initial examination, the ghost of Delmar Harper returned to hang in the air like a stain, but he stayed blessedly quiet. After a moment more, he floated away in the direction Molly had gone earlier.

"I guess we're done here," Ernie said as the attendants loaded the body onto a litter to carry it away. "Poor, foolish Delly. May you rest in peace."

"Done? Aren't you going to go up and take a look around? Seems like you should at least make sure nothing hinky happened before you mark his death as an accident."

"Delly fell. Nothing hinky about that. Maybe you should sign up for the academy since you're so interested in taking over my job."

"I'm not—" Before I could make amends, Molly popped her head up as if she'd heard someone call her name and yanked her leash out of Drew's hand. "There she goes again."

Good girl, I thought, as I took off after her in the direction I wanted to go anyway. Drew and Ernie followed. At least now, we'd all get a chance to see what was what.

The trail wound around chunks of slate deemed unusable for whatever reason and left to litter the canyon floor before circling up a relatively shallow embankment. The spot where the Jackson place bordered on the quarry must have been the end where the cache of usable slate petered out, or maybe the Jackson's land butted into the mine somehow.

Either way, the quarry floor sloped up enough that unlike the spot Christine had wanted to throw me off, Delly's fall hadn't been from all that high up. High enough to kill him, but maybe not so high he had a lot of time to be scared on the way down.

A small mercy, but one I appreciated even if it did nothing to ease my increasing fear of falling.

"The town should have made Barrow's put up gates around the perimeter before they shut down operations." Ernie gazed balefully down into the shallow end of the pit. "Delly's isn't the first body we've pulled out of there and probably won't be the last." He turned to meet the question in my eyes. "Jumpers. None local, mind you, but if you're planning to go out, there's no turning back once you step off the edge."

I shuddered, and Drew's face lost a little color as well.

"Delly wouldn't have," I said with conviction. He wouldn't have come to me otherwise, which I'll admit was pure assumption on my part.

A moment passed before Ernie said, "Hard to know what goes through a person's mind." I suspected the noncommittal response had as much to do with it having been Ernie's sister who tried to throw me into the quarry last year as it did with Delly.

I wanted to help the dead guy...well, want might be a strong word...I mean, given a choice between being haunted or not, not's gonna win out every single time, but the way he'd died poked hard at a raw nerve. When Drew dragged me out to this godforsaken spot to face my fears, a freak reenactment scenario probably wasn't what he'd had in mind.

At the top of the trail, we skirted along the edge of the ravine—me hanging a bit farther back than the men but still close enough to see the unbroken ground running in all directions.

"Look, no holes. There goes your theory he was digging too close to the edge." Which also begged the question of why Delly had let me think that's exactly what he'd been doing. He hadn't lied because the dead can't except, I guessed, by omission.

Ernie remained unconvinced. "There's also no evidence of a struggle. For all we know, he stepped on a nest of ground bees and ran the wrong way." When he saw the look on my face, he sighed and said, "I'll ask the medical examiner to run a tox screen, see if Delly'd been tipping the cup. Even if he was, without evidence of foul play, I'm leaning toward this being an accident."

Since I couldn't give a credible argument otherwise, I had to be satisfied with that.

"Fine. I'll just go get the cat now. Drew, do you think you could go and get the car? Seems like having it here would be easier than trying to hike back out carrying a cat."

Noting the stubborn set of my chin, Drew didn't try to change my mind. "I'll be right back." He headed back down the way we'd come up while I followed Ernie toward the house. I ended taking a bit of a detour when Molly dragged me off to have a pee along the edge of the fence I assumed divided Jackson land from Barrow's.

Near Molly's chosen spot, I saw a longer trench, also freshly dug. Delly certainly had been busy.

Old farmhouses in the northeast often feel as if they grew in place rather than were built. Many sprawled out one addition at a time over generations as families grew and more space became needed.

Sided mostly in cedar shingles weathered to a silvery-gray, the Jackson place looked as if it had been a victim of the reverse of that process, with sections having been hacked off and whittled down to its present state. Here and there, random cuts of aged plywood jigsawed together to cover raw spots and keep out the elements. Time had scoured off any trace of paint that ever graced the trim around windows and doors, leaving the wood to sprout deep grooves and wrinkles.

I tied Molly's leash around a post driven into the ground near the door for some unfathomable reason.

"I'll just get the cat, okay. It shouldn't take long," I said to Ernie. "Unless the door's locked."

If it was, I could dump the cat responsibility on Ernie's shoulders, and Delly couldn't fault me for that, could he?

Reaching past me like he knew what he'd find, Ernie twisted the knob and gave the door a push. "It's not locked. Delly didn't believe in locking people out. Said someone might show up needing shelter when he wasn't home. He was the least selfish man I ever met."

Didn't want to share the gold if he found it, though—I had that straight from the ghost's mouth.

Based on the outside, I expected the inside to be straight out of the pages of Early American Hovel magazine, but there, Delly surprised me.

The front door opened into one large room that

functioned as a combination of a living room and kitchen—both spaces as neat as a pin and with an unexpectedly cozy feel. Every square inch of the hardwood floor that I could see gleamed as if plenty of time went into keeping it polished.

From the outside in, his place was like night and day, and yes, I am aware his house made the perfect metaphor for the man himself. Not much to look at but inside beat a heart of solid gold. That'll teach me to judge people based on looks.

I'd have liked to look around more, but it didn't seem wise with Ernie watching.

"There's the cat." Ernie broke into my thoughts and pointed to Pearl. She blinked green eyes at me from the spot where she draped over the back of the sofa. "She looks friendly enough."

"Hey, pretty girl," I cooed. Ernie rolled his eyes, and I swear the cat did, too. But when I went closer, she tipped her head up to let me scratch under her chin. "I guess you're coming home with me now."

I felt sorry that she'd be disrupted from her home and that she'd never see Delly again, and mostly because I had no way of explaining why. She let me pick her up, which I thought was a good sign—right up until Molly tugged her hastily tied leash off the post and beelined inside.

At first, the dog didn't notice the cat in my arms, but the cat certainly saw the dog. Her claws pierced my skin deeply, her body went rigid, and she hissed her displeasure.

"Ouch! Molly! Back off, now." Fur standing up along her spine, Molly almost did as I said but didn't go far enough for the cat to relax her grip on my arm.

Okay, this was going to get interesting.

Grinning at my discomfort, Ernie grabbed Molly's leash and took her back outside. As soon as the door closed behind him, Pearl shot out of my arms, giving an extra dig with her claws on the way, and slithered under the sofa.

"Fine. You stay there while I look for a box or something." Beads of blood welled up from where she'd made her assault. "And maybe some bandages."

By the time Drew arrived, I'd amassed a pile of cat paraphernalia.

"What's all this?" he asked as I carried out the first load of stuff.

"Litter box, litter, food—both dry and wet, toys,

comb and brush, two collars. This was one spoiled cat."

Finally, with everything stashed in the trunk, we fished Pearl out from under the sofa without her drawing more blood and put her in the carrier I'd found in the back of a closet. For once, it would have helped to have the ghost around to direct, but Delly never showed.

I didn't see him again for several days. Just long enough to think maybe he'd gone into the light.

The people part of the car ride home passed mostly in silence. The pets made up for the lack of conversation. I sat in the back with Pearl in the cat carrier while Molly rode shotgun. Every few seconds, a bloodcurdling yowl rent the air, followed by an answering bark from the front seat.

About halfway there, Drew said, "Are you okay?" His gaze met mine in the rearview mirror, and I saw genuine concern, but also something else. Disappointment, maybe. I couldn't really tell.

I shrugged. "I will be." The cat yowled again, I winced, Drew winced. Molly barked.

When we got back to my place, Drew didn't offer to stay. He helped me get the cat inside, kissed me, and then left me to face my new roommate alone. I wasn't sure whether to think him wise or a coward. Or both.

# CHAPTER THREE

I don't know why I expected a smaller turnout for Delly's funeral, and to be honest, I feel bad that I underestimated his impact on the town. At least a hundred people filed in through the cemetery gates, some dressed in black, others in whatever they'd worn to work, but Delly didn't mind. Sober-faced, he stood by the urn holding his ashes and watched the procession of mourners come to pay their respects, which couldn't have been easy for him.

The service was short, and Delly had gone by the time the preacher finished and then asked if anyone wanted to speak.

"I remember this one time when Delly dickered a deal on an old John Deere tractor with a loader bucket off a fella over in Harmony. It wasn't much to look at, but it ran good and didn't need a thing. I figured he was gonna use it to dig up at the Jackson place, but he asked me to haul it home with my trailer, so I did." This from a rawboned fella in whose name I couldn't quite dredge up.

"We got back to town, and when I went to turn up toward the quarry, Delly told me to keep going. See, he knew my tractor had broke down the week before, and I needed it more than he did. He gave me a fair price on it, told me to pay him back over time, and not to be in any big rush about it, either."

Toward the end of his tale, Able Gallow—I'd finally put a name to the face—choked up and when he said, "Good man. I'll miss him." I teared up because he did.

Another man stepped up to speak. "Every year come harvest time, Delly showed up on my doorstep offering to help pick potatoes. He never took a dime for the work, only a fifty-pound bag at the end of the week, and he did more work than any two of my hired hands." He paused and smiled a little. "Talked more than any of them, too."

Then a woman cleared her throat. "I haven't lived in Mooselick River as long as the rest of you, so I've only known Delly for about five years, but I'll never forget the first time I almost met him. It wasn't too long after my husband passed, and I was feeling pretty low, to begin with. It was the first snowstorm of the season, and I couldn't get the snowblower started." She sniffed back tears and smiled.

"There I was, shoveling the end of the driveway, bawling, and cursing the fates when Delly pulled up in that old rattletrap truck of his. He dropped the plow, took two swipes to clean me out, then tipped me a smile, and drove off without giving me a chance to even say thank you."

Heads nodded, I heard sniffling, and someone said, "That was Delly. Always ready with a helping hand."

Someone else said, "And a good joke if you needed to hear one."

The stories went on for a solid hour, during which I realized the town had lost more than just one of its more colorful characters. Though he'd had little of material means, Delly had contributed to his community by giving of himself. More people should be like him, and I made a vow to find his killer no matter what it took.

To that end, I eased my way to a position where I could see more of the crowd and watched faces as more and more people came forward with stories about the deceased. Amid the tear-stained, one set of dry eyes stood out. Carlene Nicholson rolled her hazel-colored ones toward the sky every time someone said something nice.

I knew from personal experience that Carlene could carry a grudge like a Prada handbag, so what was her beef with Delly? And was it worth subjecting myself to her acid presence to find out?

Of course, I decided it was, so I moved slowly in her direction. Before I could reach her, a short, bespectacled man appeared, took her arm, and pulled her away for a brief conversation that ended in her throwing back her head to emit a laugh that jarred the general atmosphere of grieving.

"No. I'm not interested. Just leave me out of it, okay?"

He nodded, and while I didn't hear what he said, I assume he asked her to follow him to his car. She did, and I did what any good sleuth would do: pretended to need something from my car. I maintained my distance and thanked my lucky stars he'd parked close enough for me to hear a bit of what was said.

"If you could sign here, Ms. Nicholson."

She did; he thanked her, stowed the papers, and walked back toward Delly's memorial. After a short pause, Carlene did the same, her path taking her right past me.

When Carlene noticed me there, she didn't look happy. "If it isn't the prodigal cheerleader." Did the air feel cooler as I got closer to her? Seemed like it to me.

"Hi, Carlene. I'm surprised to see you here." And somewhat dismayed, but I didn't tell her that.

She gave me the once over, her gaze sweeping down to my feet then back up to my face.

"I don't see why not. I," she glanced back toward the table that held the urn, "I'm the only family he had left."

"Really? I had no idea."

"Well, there's a wealth of things you know nothing about, now isn't there, Everly Dupree?"

Carlene said my name in about the same tone she might have used for calling me something nasty, and I had to bite back a comment of my own. Now was not the time or place for feuding over old offenses— real or imagined.

"Probably," I shrugged off the insult and persisted. "How were you and Delly related?" In my head, I did a quick spate of math to see if he could possibly have been her father. If so, I'd have pitied him even more.

Settling her hands on her hips, Carlene tilted her

head. "If you must know, Delly was my step-cousin." She paused and tacked on, "Once removed."

Okay, I'm just going to admit right here that the whole *so many times removed* thing mystifies me completely. My grandmother tried to explain it to me more than once, but I still don't get it. Did it even apply to step-relatives?

"On your mother's side or your father's?"

I got the eye-roll again and a flip of tawny hair behind one ear to go with it.

"My grandmother married Delly's uncle when my father was barely out of diapers. That makes us step-cousins once removed."

"Do you mean Clint Jackson? I know he was Delly's uncle, but I was under the impression he'd never married."

"Not him. There were three in that family. Clint, a sister, and a brother." Altering her tone to that of someone talking to the not-so-bright, she emphasized. "My step-grandfather."

"Okay, fine. I get it." I mocked her tone and then felt bad about it because this was a funeral and for a relative—or at least a near relative—of hers, even if she seemed not to be the least bit upset.

None of what she said explained the once

removed part, but I wasn't about to ask Carlene for clarification. "So, you're not really related to Delly at all, then." I meant by blood and didn't realize how stupid I sounded until I heard the words come out of my mouth. "I'm sorry. I didn't mean it like that. Are there other cousins?"

Considering her bored demeanor throughout the service, there didn't seem to be any love lost between the cousins, no matter what family configuration had brought them together.

"Didn't I just say I was his only relative?" Carlene's expression actually brightened. "But as I just told that lawyer fellow, we weren't anything to each other, and I'm not paying for his funeral." She trilled a laugh at me over her shoulder as she left me staring after her. "Everyone in town thought he was a saint; let them all chip in for it."

I'd once apologized to Carlene when she gave me the impression I'd done or said something to hurt her feelings when we were younger. Now, I wasn't sure she had any feelings at all, and while I didn't regret making the apology, there would be no reiteration of it should we meet again.

"Sorry, Delly," I muttered in case he lingered nearby. "You didn't make out too well in the relative pool." Which begged the question of who *had* paid for Delly's funeral. I wasn't sure who to ask but added the question to my list if I ever figured it out. The more I knew, the better chance of figuring out what happened to him.

While I'd had my conversation with the Wicked Witch of the East, most of the mourners had gone, so I drifted over to join my mother. She stood a little way apart from where my father carried on an earnest conversation with three men, one of them the man Carlene had identified as Delly's lawyer.

"Is this it? Or will there be a gathering somewhere else?" There was usually food after these types of things or a wake of sorts. According to Carlene, Delly hadn't had any family left to throw a wake, and she certainly hadn't stepped up. How sad.

"Not today, but we've planned a bean supper for a week from Saturday to raise money for a headstone. Martha wrangled a discounted price from the mortuary. If the supper doesn't raise enough, she said she'd use some of the money from the town's emergency fund to cover the balance."

"I expect I'll be getting a phone call from Martha to help drum up more support." Since my less-than-triumphant return home, I'd been using my organizational skills to help Martha in her endeavors to bring Mooselick River back to its former glory. "That guy talking to dad—"

"We were getting ready to leave when that fellow showed up. He said he was Delly's attorney of record, then asked to speak to your father in private." Graceful as ever, my mom used her chin to gesture toward the group of men. "I heard the words Will and Testament, but I couldn't make out anything after that."

My mom is the town librarian, so information is kind of her thing. Not knowing something is her Kryptonite. Being cut out of that conversation must have been driving her nuts.

"Delly had a will? He never—" I cut myself off before I dug a verbal hole I couldn't yank myself out of. I'd never found the right time to tell my parents about my ghostly visitations, and now wasn't the time, either. "Don't you think it's odd he'd show up today? I mean, Delly didn't have much to leave anyone, did he?"

"Not anymore," my mother said. Before I could ask for clarification, the group broke up, and my father, a tall man with prematurely gray hair and kind eyes, walked toward us.

As if he needed to breathe, he loosened his tie, popped the top button of his shirt open, and pulled the collar away from his neck. In the heat of an early summer sun, anyone might find a black suit a bit too warm, but not enough to redden his face so much. He didn't offer one of his soothing hugs, and his hair had gone poofy the way it always did when he felt upset or agitated.

Never let it be said Kitty Dupree wasted words when a look could do the trick.

"Delly named me in his will," my father confirmed with a twist of his lips. "I'm his Executor."

That one came as a shock. "Why would he pick you for that?"

"Because, and this is a direct quote, I'm the best man he knows."

Mom smiled and reached out to lay her hand on his cheek. "Delly was a good judge of character. If I remember correctly, he didn't have any family left, and I'm sure he knew you would honor his wishes."

My parents are romantically sappy sometimes. I like that about them.

"He did have family, though. Carlene Nicholson was his step-cousin." For once, I had more information than my mother.

Dad backed me up. "That's right, but Delly anticipated her reaction and stipulated that if she refused to take on the job, the honor would default to me."

"Oh, she refused all right," I repeated everything Carlene had told me. When I got to the once removed part, my mother frowned. Maybe she didn't get it, either.

"Refused is a mild word for what she did," Dad's face set in disapproving lines. "When I asked if she might reconsider, she said she'd rather have her nails chewed off by a rabid dog than oversee Delly's final wishes."

"She's a—" At a look from my mother, I bit back the word I wanted to use. "Well, she is. I'm sorry the onus falls on you, Dad, but I know you'll do a better job of sorting through Delly's personal effects than she ever would. She couldn't have cared less for him."

After checking to make sure there wasn't anyone else within hearing distance, my father said, "How do you think she'd have felt about going on a treasure hunt?"

Since I couldn't begin to dredge up the mental image of Carlene picking up a shovel, much less knowing which end to use to dig a hole, I snorted.

"I suspect there would be a great lack of enthusiasm. Why?"

"Delly designated a small group of friends as beneficiaries of the only thing he thought he had of value." Dad dropped the bomb. "He wants us to find Clint's gold, and he put me in charge of the hunt."

It's a rare thing to see my mother stunned, but that did it. "You're kidding."

"I wish I were."

"Leland Bennett Dupree. If you think I'm spending my summer vacation watching you dig holes all over some Godforsaken piece of property because Delmar Harper thinks you're smart, you'd better think again."

Mom's hands landed on her hips, and fire lit her eyes. "I saved up my personal days and my allotted vacation time for the entire year so I could have a full four weeks this summer. We have plans. You need to tell that cousin of his she's going to do her duty whether she likes it or not."

"Calm down, Kitty."

Telling my mother to calm down had about the same level of effect as telling the rain to stop falling, but before she could wind up for another volley, he said, "Delly hadn't paid the taxes on the property yet, and since we're at the end of our town's fiscal year, I have—as Executor—made the decision to limit the festivities until the tax books close next week and the property semi-officially becomes the town's problem."

"That's okay, then." Mom's good humor returned. "Should I start shopping for a European tour in case you strike it rich?"

"Can I go with you?" My abrupt question stopped the conversation.

"To Europe?" Mom frowned.

"No." It occurred to me that if the gold really did exist, it could provide a motive for Delly's death. I couldn't tell my parents I meant to hunt down a killer, so I looked down at my feet and said, "To look for the gold." Embarrassed heat pinked my cheeks, making me curse, and as always, the pale skin that came along with my red hair betrayed me.

I just hate it when my parents exchange amused looks over something I've done. It makes me feel like a teenager all over again.

## CHAPTER FOUR

The day after the funeral, Molly forgot her manners and yanked me into a jog for the last half block of our walk back from the park. I figured she was trying to get away from Delly, who'd followed us since we left the house.

Or was that just me?

"Willard Tucker lives right here. I bought a car off him once. A little Ford Festiva—can't remember the year. Little hatchback. Ran real nice. I drove it near on two years. This one time, I hit a bump over near Slopes Corner, and the back window fell right clean out of her. Cost me a pretty penny to get it fixed. Only kept liability on it, so nothing like that was covered."

Ghosts don't have to breathe, and Delly took advantage of the perk by not shutting his mouth all the way to the park and back. It was no wonder Molly had had enough.

But when my driveway came in sight, I realized

her reason had more to do with the truck parked there than escaping Delly's slightly nasal voice.

"Looks like I've got company." I hoped the ghost would take the hint.

He did. "I guess I'll make myself scarce then." I almost expected Delly's smile to linger after he was gone like the Cheshire cat. How someone could kill such a jolly man whose only crime seemed to be talking too much was a mystery to me. You couldn't help but like him, so I couldn't imagine what he'd done to earn such a horrible fate.

David Barrington ranked as one of Molly's favorite people and not just because he carried bacon-flavored dog treats in his pockets sometimes. He also had unlimited patience for tossing a slobber-coated tennis ball.

The anticipation of either or both of those things led the dog right up to the driver's side door of the truck where I could see David resting his head on his arms which he'd folded over the steering wheel.

"What's wrong? Are you hurt?" I let go of Molly's leash and leaned as far as I could through the window to check for bruises or bleeding. Seeing none, my mind immediately went somewhere else. "Is it your parents? Or mine?"

David's father and mine were old friends, which is how, after a personal tragedy, David had come to be staying with my parents when I moved back to town. At the time, I'd been annoyed, but he eventually won me over, and we'd become friends.

"No. No one is hurt." His voice sounded muffled. "Except maybe my pride." Without lifting his head, he turned it and presented me with a baffled, one-eyed look. One I recognized. "I just bought the Marlow."

"She wore you down," I crowed. "You totally got Martha'd!"

When I'd moved back to town with almost nothing to my name, Martha Tipton had done me the solid favor of gently pushing me to purchase Willowby house—formerly known as Spooky Manor—and its contents for the ridiculously small sum owed on back taxes. Given that the house had been well-maintained, came fully furnished with a car in the garage, and cost me roughly what I'd have spent on first, last, and security on an apartment, I'd made out very well in the bargain. I'd owe Martha a debt for life.

Over the past few months, she'd been working on David to purchase the Marlow Inn. Unlike me, David was a no impulse-shopper, especially when it came to buying a rambling, three-story piece of ginger-bread architecture in an unknown state of habitability. My place had only sat empty for a year and needed cleaning. The Marlow had been closed for a lot longer.

"I knew she'd wear you down eventually." The bones of the old inn—and I knew what the term meant now that I was a homeowner myself—were sound. It had been built to last, but the plumbing and electrical needed upgrading, and those things packed definite money-pit potential. David had decided the inn required more work than he wanted to tackle and had told Martha his answer was no.

No is a word that lives far outside of Martha's vocabulary.

David lifted his head and stepped out of the truck. "I'm not even sure how it happened. I went to the town office to re-glaze a window, and then I was at the bank asking Bill Cavanaugh if my pre-approval for the loan was still good. Everything in the middle is a blur."

He hunched over like a puppy being chastised for piddling on the floor. "If you ask me, Cavanaugh and Martha are in cahoots. He was in an awful hurry to put the paperwork through. Shouldn't it take at least a week or two, even a month for something like this?"

I shrugged. "I can only go by my own experience, and mine took almost a week because it was a cash deal, and I couldn't get the keys until the title was filed. Jacy's took a couple of months because the closing got delayed a few times, but she got the keys that day. I think the process varies."

Pressing a palm to his forehead as if to stop an ache, David nodded. "Maybe since we'd already done some of the paperwork when I originally applied, it was easy to expedite now. Bill said it was a foreclosure property, and he put the loan through in half an hour." He pulled a set of keys out of his pocket, jingling them at me.

Figuring he needed coffee—or maybe something stronger—I hid a smirk, took David's arm, and led him inside with Molly following behind. "Martha probably called ahead and told him you were a flight risk given how long it took her to talk you into saying yes once she decided you were the right person for the Marlow."

On this occasion, I agreed with Martha. David paid attention to detail and enjoyed working with his hands. The inn needed someone who would restore it rather than demolish or renovate. Someone who cared about retaining the history of the place. The inn needed David, but even more, I think David needed the inn to help him heal some of his own broken places.

Giving his arm a squeeze, I said, "Look, you've been waffling over this decision for months now, and you know if someone else had swooped in and snatched it off the market, you'd have lived with the regret of second-guessing yourself. Martha did you a favor by nudging you along. We'll have a celebratory lunch, and then we'll go take another look at the place."

"You're gloating," David reached out and tugged on a lock of my hair in the way a brother would do—we had that kind of relationship. "Because I joined the bamboozled by Martha club."

Maybe I hadn't hidden my smirk as well as I thought. "I am not. Or not much. Maybe a little. It's nice to have a new member. There's chicken and rice soup. Want grilled cheese with it? Looks like I have provolone."

"Sure." He'd let go of some of the tension, so we talked about the inn while I cooked, and then he brought up Delly Harper's untimely death.

"I'd met him a few times. Nice guy if a little…" David hesitated as if reluctant to speak ill of the dead. "Talkative."

I wanted to tell David he didn't know the half of it, but since I couldn't explain the comment, I kept it to myself.

Then he hit me with a shocker. "Did you know the Harper family used to own the Marlow?"

"I did not." My fork stopped halfway to my mouth as my mother's odd comment at the funeral became clear. "Seems like that would have been worth mentioning." Yet, the chatterbox hadn't said a word to me about it. "Fascinating."

David raised a brow at the use of such a strong word. "I saw the name in the listings for results from the title search."

"Could have been another family of Harpers." I frowned down at my soup. I'd added a little more pepper than I normally liked. "It's a common name, after all. There are plenty of Harpers scattered across the area."

"Maybe so, but I doubt there are that many with the first name of Delmar. According to what I read, it passed from Delmar senior to Delmar junior when he died. I assume Delly was junior. He held onto it until the bank foreclosed five years ago. They've been trying to auction or sell it off ever since. Probably waiting for the right sucker to come along, and here I am." David grimaced and held up a hand. "That would be me. There's one born every minute."

I rolled my eyes at him. "Here comes the pity party bus again. I went with you to look the place over the first time you thought about buying it, remember? The structure is sound; you said so yourself. It's a good investment. With the expansion up in Hackinaw not going as quickly as expected, we're seeing some overflow here in Mooselick River. We're slowly building up businesses and activities to bring in more tourism, and with the lake nearby, there's no reason why you couldn't make a go of it with an inn or cozy B&B."

His plate rattled against the tabletop when David pushed it away. "Martha Tipton is pure evil," he announced. "Do I look like the cozy innkeeper type?"

"No," I had to admit. "Not exactly, but that's a detail in the landscape. You could hire a manager or just fix it up and sell the place for a profit. If you're really worried about it, you have three days to change your mind, right?"

I thought I'd made a positive statement, but David didn't take it that way.

"And what? Renege on a deal? I'm a Barrington, and we're not welshers."

A Wimbledon tennis match went back and forth less than David.

"Okay! I get it. What's done is done. Let's go and start figuring out how to make the best of the situation." Besides, hearing about Delly's connection to the inn had me curious to learn anything that might help get him out of my hair. The man—or ghost—could talk the ears off a brass donkey. The sooner he found his way into the light, the better.

# CHAPTER FIVE

Knowing the place had a history connected to my current mystery, I paid more attention when David opened up the doors, and we stepped into the foyer of the old inn. Call it a flight of fancy, but I thought I heard the bright sounds of a boy's laughter echo through the empty rooms. Delly would have been happy here, I thought, running up and down the stairs and exploring every nook and cranny.

"It has a good energy, don't you think? Like the people who visited here felt welcome."

"I guess it's not as bad as I remember it." David scuffed a foot on the carpet, which released a puff of dust and made me sneeze. "Needs cleaning."

"Sure," I said, "but look at those high ceilings, and isn't that pressed tin going up the stairs? I remember you waxing rhapsodic over mine once."

"Get a grip. I did not."

He certainly had, but I didn't think a round of did

not/did too was what he needed now. Hurt me to let it go, though. Instead, I took his arm, pulled him toward what I assumed had been the check-in area where a tall counter arced in a graceful curve. The wall behind the counter featured a set of mail cubbies and a board with hooks labeled for each of the eight rooms.

Whether it worked now or not, I coveted the light fixture set into a recessed ceiling over the counter with its delicate, fluted glass shade in a pearly white.

"Look at that," I drew David's attention upward.

"I know the paint's peeling."

"I meant the gorgeous light fixture."

"It's nice enough, I guess."

And that was how it went. I pointed out the beauty in the fireplace mantel's intricate detail, but David only saw the flaws. I peeled back a corner of an old rug to reveal parquet flooring underneath, and David announced they'd put the carpet down to cover up the wear and tear.

"Thousands of dollars and thousands of hours' worth of work. That's what I've taken on. What was I thinking?" He rounded on me, sheer panic tightening his face into worried lines. "I'm sunk. It's too much." His breathing hitched.

"You're having a panic attack."

"I think I am." David clutched his chest. "Or a heart attack. I can't breathe."

"Come on." I pulled him outside, settled him down on the front steps, and shoved his head down between his bent knees. "Breathe now. In and out. In and out. Slower. Deep, even breaths." I gentled my tone to as soothing as I could manage because seeing him this way scared me, too.

After a few breaths, he settled into the new pattern and began to calm down.

"It's okay to be scared. Anyone sane would be scared at taking on such a job, but this is totally in your wheelhouse, and I know you can turn this place into something great. I have faith."

"You don't understand. I have to tell you something, and you're going to be upset."

"Now you have me worried. What is it?" I put a hand on his arm.

"I want you to know I didn't ask them to do it, and I tried to talk them out of it, but your mother is almost as bad as Martha once she makes her mind up."

The mild understatement brought a smile. "Let

me guess. They wanted to invest in the inn, and you don't think they should."

"I tried to tell them no. It's a losing prospect. This place needs too much work, but they wouldn't let it go."

What an idiot. I punched him in the arm. "They aren't investing in the inn, you moron; they're investing in you. And you know what? If I had any amount of money in the bank, I'd do the same because this is a great property with a ton of potential, but that potential pales in comparison to yours."

"You're not pissed off?"

This time I only shoulder butted him as we sat side by side. "I am—but not because my parents know a good investment when they see one—because you're selling yourself short, and that's annoying. Now get your weenie butt up off these stairs, go back inside, and let's look at this place the right way. With enthusiasm."

"You're sure you're not mad?"

"Keep making me repeat myself, and we'll see how it goes. Didn't I just say I had faith? Up, now. I want to see the kitchen and the bedrooms. I might be able to give you a deal on some furniture when the time comes."

When we went back inside, I discovered we were no longer alone.

"Do you think if Delly hadn't gone and gotten himself murdered, he'd have been able to get the place fixed up? If he found the gold, I mean."

"I don't see why not. It doesn't actually need that much."

I wondered if David would pull a muscle flipping so quickly, but I grinned at him. The change of heart was good to see. He seemed lighter as I followed him upstairs to check the ceilings for signs of roof leaks.

"You're a good girl and a good friend," Delly said. At least he waited until David had gone back to his truck for a tape measure and a notebook. "You take after your grandmother."

That his tone was kindly made the comment no less of a backhanded compliment. My grandmother's tendency to speak her mind led to her being both revered and reviled by the residents of Mooselick River. Being compared to her could go either way, depending on who was doing the comparing.

She'd done her level best to instill in me the same disregard she'd felt when running afoul of criticism.

*Everly, my girl*—I could hear her voice in my head—*opinions are like belly buttons. Everyone's got one, but that don't make them special.* The first time she'd trotted out that particular adage, I'd spent hours staring at mine trying to figure out if she'd meant the belly buttons or the people.

"Thank you," I said. I was firmly in the revered column when it came to Grammie Dupree. "That means a lot."

"You have her pigheadedness, too. That woman would chew glass before she'd admit she made a mistake."

Well, that sounded less flattering.

"You think I've messed up something?" While we talked, I kept an ear out for David's return.

"I should think that between the two of us, I'm the one who ought to know if I'd been murdered or not, and I wasn't."

Otherworldly energy teased the hairs on the back of my neck and sent goosebumps prickling down my arms, but I pressed on anyway. "Not to be disrespect-ful, but you're not my first ghost, and there are rules for these sorts of things."

At least there had been up to now, so why would I assume this haunting was any different? I only saw the ghosts of people whose death was the result of mysterious or violent murder. Falling off a cliff certainly qualified as a violent death, and I didn't think it was any sort of stretch to assume Delly hadn't done so by accident.

He was still here, wasn't he? That was all the evidence I needed.

Delly did not see the situation the same way and wasn't shy about saying so.

"Okay, then. I know you weren't up there hunting treasure, so why don't you tell me what happened the day you died. But hurry, before David comes back." I tilted my head—somewhat arrogantly—and waited for him to do what every ghost before him had done: begin to tell me about their last moments, freak out, and go poof. He'd done it once already.

At least, I thought he did. Now he had me confused.

"Weren't no different from any other day," he began. "Except this time, I thought for sure I'd found the spot where Clint sunk his gold. Ten acres don't sound like much of a parcel, but it's a fair bit of land when you're turning over one shovelful of dirt at a time."

Geography has never been my strong suit. I guess you could say I'm spatially challenged because I couldn't tell ten acres from ten feet. But neither of those had anything to do with why Delly had been hanging around the quarry ledge on his last day on earth. Or I guess his last physical day on earth.

While I contemplated the semantics, he continued.

"I got up around six, ate breakfast—scrambled eggs and baloney—and went to digging. Same as I do every day except for the eggs. Sometimes I like them over easy and sometimes fried hard. Pearl likes a bit of cheese in hers, but I take mine with ketchup, and I always put three cuts in my baloney to get it to lay flat in the pan. Mabel over at the diner only does one, but you probably knew that."

I went to the window, looked down to see David still sorting through things in his truck, and circled a hand to get Delly to talk faster and get to the point.

"I need you to be clear. Were you planning to dig near the quarry, and did anyone know where you'd be working that day?"

"Not to the best of my recollection. Do you think I didn't know what people said behind my back?" Delly rolled his eyes and mock-sneered. "There goes that Delly Harper chasing rainbows and fool's gold again."

"Don't let it get you down. People have nothing

better to do than talk sometimes." I'd been the topic of more than one conversation since I'd returned to town. Probably a few before I left, too.

Based on what he had said so far, I could only assume he'd been planning to dig in the area but hadn't had a chance to get started. That meant he'd probably died earlier in the day than I'd initially thought.

"But there must be someone who knew how to find you. Are you sure you didn't talk to anyone about where you'd be? Even in passing?"

"It's nice of you to want to help, and if I'm stuck here, I don't mind saying I'm darned glad to have a warm soul to talk to, but you're chasing the wrong dog. I always did my best to be neighborly, just like my daddy taught me. Ain't no one in this town ever been mad enough to toss me off a cliff."

And yet, here he was, in all his ghostly glory, so I begged to differ. "What happened next?"

He described—in great detail—how he'd picked out the tree that would be his starting point, paced out the distance according to Clint's accounting of the burial spot, and then marked out the beginnings of what would become a semi-circular dig pattern around the tree.

"You've got to have a method to the madness with these things. I can't rightly say how tall Clint was, and a hundred and fifty paces isn't an accurate measure of distance when you have to account for the length of a man's leg."

Despite myself, I began to get interested in the way Delly's mind worked. He'd certainly put a lot of effort into coming up with a logical approach to the details over the years.

By his own estimate, he'd dug over a thousand holes since he'd begun searching.

"In all that time, you found nothing. What made you keep going?" You had to give the man credit for determination.

Delly grinned. "What else was I supposed to do?" Then he turned pensive. "I don't have a head for numbers or business, so I lost the inn. Finding Clint's gold was the only chance I had to get it back. I guess it's too late now."

David's truck door slammed.

"If it helps, you should know David will take excellent care of the inn. It needs some updating, mostly mechanical—plumbing, electrical, and whatnot—but he's planning to use the original fixtures where he can and reproductions where he can't. When it's done, it should be very much like you remember."

Delly closed his eyes, and I swear I saw a ghostly tear well up in the corner of his eye before he nodded and took back control of his emotions.

"I hope he does."

"Now, quick before he comes back. The day I found you, you said you saw someone before you fell. Who?"

"Oh, that was nothing. Just the lady in red."

David's feet hit the bottom step, and Delly poofed again, leaving me to wonder who he meant. Just one more layer to the mystery.

## CHAPTER SIX

The great treasure hunt got pushed a day on account of rain, which turned out well for me since I ended up having to work. My job managing rental properties pays well enough, and the hours are more than flexible. Half the time, it barely feels like work at all, and then there are the days like this one that really kind of suck.

I'd barely had a chance to look things over before Delly turned up to talk my ear off. He flat refused to discuss his death again, leaving me with no other option but to let him chatter and hope he unwittingly dropped useful information.

"Would you look at this place? I didn't know Leo kept things up so nice. Must be why he charges an arm, a leg, and the moon for rent. This house is fit for a king."

I tried to tune out Delly's voice with little success. Compared to his place, the house on Tulip—vacant again as of the first of the month—was the nicer of the two, but I wouldn't have gone so far as to say it was a palace. It certainly didn't look like one now.

Armed with a bucket, broom, mop, and huge tote of cleaning supplies, I had a full day of work ahead of me. We'd rented the place to Leo's nephew and family when his out-of-state job transfer got delayed a month after they'd already sold their home.

Who would have thought three people could generate so much filth in such a short time?

Thinking it best to start at the top, I filled the bucket with hot, soapy water, carried it upstairs, and went back down for the tote. Most of the time, I find cleaning to be cathartic. Satisfying, even. This day, the process only annoyed.

Looking at the corners of the bedrooms, I had to wonder if they'd imported some species of spider with the superpower of making webs at warp speed. Before I tackled the tangled mess with my trusty broom, I tied a bandana over my head.

Hey, I'm no shrinking violet, but the idea of spiders crawling around in my hair gives me the shivers.

"This house used to belong to Ken Monroe. Poor

old fella. His heart gave out on him. Must have been fifteen years ago, I recollect. Dropped down dead at the feed store over in Dover. They say he was gone before he hit the ground."

Delly was like a walking obituary.

"That's too bad." My brief answer wasn't enough to deter the rest of the story.

"Wasn't no surprise there. Old Ken ate a can of Spam and half a pound of bacon for breakfast every morning for thirty years. It's a wonder he made it to eighty-three."

There was more, but it seemed a nod of acknowledgment, and an absent mumble was enough to keep Delly happy. While he provided more detail about the former owner than I ever wanted to know, I cleared the cobwebs, brushed the dust off the walls, and decided that if the grubby fingerprints came off the door trim, this bedroom at least, could get by without needing a fresh coat of paint.

"—mother was a seamstress." For all I knew, Delly was still talking about Ken whatever his name was, but even he stopped when a loud knocking sounded at the front door. The ghost beat me down the stairs, but then again, he didn't need to worry about slipping on the carpet. Or about doors since he poked his head right through to see who'd knocked.

"It's that real estate woman," he pulled his head back and spoke over his shoulder but didn't get out of my way. Touching ghosts feels like touching cold slime. It makes the hairs on the back of my neck stand up and dance. I don't like it.

"You know, the one from all the signs."

She knocked again and confirmed Delly's observation by calling through the door. "Hello, anyone in there. It's Maryann Payne." She knocked again, louder.

"I'm coming." In a lower voice, I said, "Delly, could you please move?"

He got out of my way, but reluctantly, and he didn't go far as I opened the door a crack.

"Hi," I said, and wanting to keep the interruption to a minimum, didn't step back. "What can I do for you?"

Maryann's smile seemed genuine, her eyes crinkling enough to show the beginnings of crow's feet as she introduced herself and handed me a card. When I opened my mouth to try and get rid of her, she held up a hand and cut me off.

"I know Leo's not interested in selling this place,

but I'm listing a house down the street and putting together some comps—that's a list of comparable properties, by the way. Leo's made a lot of improvements here. I was hoping to come in and take a look around. You don't mind, do you?"

"Actually, I've got—" I was going to say a lot of cleaning to do, but it was already too late. Determined, Maryann tossed her head, her short wedge of hair—dyed a few shades too dark for her skin tone—never moved. She looked like everyone's favorite auntie but still somehow gave me the impression of a pit-bull in a business suit over running shoes. She pushed past me and marched inside.

Still wearing the rubber gloves I'd donned before picking up what appeared to be a solid half box of used nose tissue from the bedroom closet floor, and helpless to stop the intrusion, I followed along behind.

"Built by Jonas Brandywine for the textile mill's department managers back in the late eighteen hundreds," Maryann went into lecture mode. "Only three of the original five remain. One burned down in 1927, and one was demolished in the seventies after it fell into disrepair."

"Interesting," I lied. "Listen, I've got—" I tried

again, and again managed to get no further. The only plus side to the invasion was that after the real estate agent had walked right through him without so much as a shudder, Delly had taken himself off to wherever it is he went when he wasn't talking a blue streak at me.

Stumpy legs flashing, Maryann made her way through the downstairs at a surprisingly fast pace. "Tsk. Tsk," she clacked her tongue against the roof of her mouth. "I warned Leo about renting to just any Tom, Dick, or Harry that comes along. Becoming a landlord is a thankless business, and quite often, less than profitable."

"Leo does okay," I defended my boss, a frugal and unassuming man who had managed to amass what most in our small town would consider a fortune. Well, unassuming until he declared his love for the owner of the Blue Moon Cafe in a public and musical manner. Since then, he'd grown enough of a backbone that people looked at him differently.

Maryann's chin went up, she gave me a half-smile, and poked herself in the chest with one thumb. "I suspect we have very different ideas about what doing okay means. I'm on track to log a million dollars' worth of listings this year."

When the state altered the road system so tourist traffic bypassed the town on the way to Hackinaw, they dealt Mooselick River what might possibly be a death blow. The town began to shrink—businesses closed; people put their homes up for sale and moved away.

The exodus launched real estate into a buyer's market, which drove prices to an all-time low. Maryann's brag, while it sounded impressive, wasn't such a mean feat. Listings weren't a guarantee of sales. However, it wasn't my place to take the woman down a peg or two.

"Impressive," I said with as much sincerity as I could muster. It must have been enough because she smiled and practically bounced up the stairs. Her footsteps raced from room to room, and she was already on her way back down before I'd decided whether or not to follow.

"You know, this place isn't bad at all—under the grime, I mean." And then she got down to her real reason for knocking on the door. "What's Leo getting for rent on a two-bedroom house these days?"

It wasn't like she was asking for secret information, so I gave her the number and noted the speculative lift of one eyebrow as she did some mental math.

Whatever she'd come here for, I saw the moment she changed tack.

"Listen, you tell Leo to call me if he's looking for another rental house. The one down the street would be perfect. It's the mirror image layout of this one and only needs a little TLC. And you can tell him I'm looking for a quick turnover on it, but he'd better not make too lowball an offer, okay? The sellers are motivated but not desperate."

I agreed to pass the message along and figured she'd leave, but she lingered.

"Was there something else?" I had rooms to clean, and we were burning daylight.

"Must have been scary finding Delmar Harper's body." Maryann proved she knew who I was. Just great. But if she thought she was the first one to try fishing in that particular gossip pool, Ms. Payne was very much mistaken, and I wasn't biting.

"It didn't rank right up there in my top ten best days." I deflected since I didn't really want to go over the details with a virtual stranger. "I'm sorry, Maryann, but I have a lot of work to do to get this place shipshape in time to show to prospective tenants in the morning."

Anyone with a shred of dignity would have taken

the hint, but not Maryann. Nope. Maryann merely grinned and offered to help. An offer which, at any other time, I'd have been grateful to accept.

"Uh, no." I stammered. "There's no need. I'm good."

"Pish tosh," her voice went up in a lilt.

What did that even mean?

"I have a couple of hours to kill, and I can show you a sweet little trick for getting magic marker off of hardwood floors."

"There's magic marker on the floors?" I hadn't seen any, but her eagle eye missed nothing. There didn't seem to be much I could do to dissuade her, so I mustered up some grace, gave in, and followed Maryann back upstairs.

Grammie Dupree would have cautioned me about looking gift horses in the mouth.

But then again, Grammie Dupree was a wise woman who also said the Devil always takes back his gifts. And so, while I appreciated the help, I didn't exactly trust Maryann's motives.

I did, however, have to admire her alacrity. The woman set about the cleaning with a cheerful and single-minded vengeance. She didn't try to tease more information out of me but chattered endlessly about each of her current listings. And her trick with magic marker worked like a charm.

"It's the alcohol," Maryann said as she squirted hand sanitizer on the floor. "I always keep a bottle of this stuff in my purse."

Based on the size of said purse, Maryann carried a lot of things around with her at all times.

"I suppose it's good to be prepared, and I'll remember the tip," I said. "Looks like we're done up here. I appreciate the help." She'd saved me half a day of hard slog, so it wasn't hard to warm up to the woman, and I could see where she'd be effective at her job. You couldn't help but feel the type of comfortable around her that would lead to sales.

Back downstairs, she still didn't leave and tackled the living room while I took care of the kitchen—only poking her head in once to make a face when she saw me dropping plastic food containers directly from the refrigerator into the trash.

"Seems like a waste," she said.

"You want to open them, you go right ahead and be my guest."

A laugh trilled out of her. "Oh, that's okay. I have plenty."

When she finally left, I hauled the trash out to the

curb, cracked open a kitchen window, and set the oven to the self-cleaning cycle. The place looked habitable again, and no small thanks to Maryann.

I called Leo to alert him to the upcoming listing, and to update him on my progress, then headed home to spend the evening with my boyfriend, my dog, and the new cat. And pizza. I'd earned it.

## CHAPTER SEVEN

"How soon can you be here?" Martha Tipton didn't bother to say hello back the next morning when I answered my phone.

"I'm signing a lease right now, then I have to drop the paperwork off with Leo. Now's not a good time." Besides, I was already running late for my date at the Jackson place to check in with my dad and his merry band of gold hunters.

I could almost hear the older woman building up a head of steam. "You tell Leo he'll have to wait. We need to get on top of this opportunity before it's too late. Now, how soon," Martha spaced out her words for emphasis. "Can you be here?"

Just for a second, I closed my eyes and wished I'd never bailed Martha out of that first bind with the town festival. Once I'd given her a taste of my party planning and organizational skills, she'd been a constant bundle of need ever since. And I owed her one for getting me into my house, let's not forget that less than small favor, I reminded myself. Eventually, Martha might earn that favor out, but not just yet.

On top of all that, my head felt full of fuzzy sludge. Drew had canceled on me at the last minute the night before using a lame excuse that set off alarm bells. They rang all night, making it difficult to sleep.

"Where's here?" I held back a sigh. "The town office?"

"Naturally." As soon as Martha knew she had me, her voice went up an octave. "I think we have an opportunity on our hands, and we don't have much time, so get here as soon as you can."

Undoubtedly, the opportunity equaled another hair-brained scheme to draw people into Mooselick River, where they would, hopefully, spend some of their hard-earned money. On principle, I agreed with the need. In reality, we'd done enough functions over the past year that I was running out of favors to call in for whatever last-minute miracle Martha deemed necessary.

The woman was more than twice my age, but keeping up with her was enough to tire out the Energizer bunny.

When I rolled into the parking lot half an hour later, the front windows looked like a people aquarium with faces pressed up against the glass. Bess Tate, Martha, and Patricia Croft, the third of the unholy trio, had been watching for me. I barely resisted the temptation to throw the car in reverse.

Martha met me at the door, put her hand on my arm to draw me inside, and said, "It's not every day we have a bona fide treasure hunt in Mooselick River."

"What does she think I've been doing all this time?" Behind me, Delly had picked the absolute worst time to pop up. But then, that's how things work in my life.

To be fair, I defended him. "Didn't Delly conduct a treasure hunt for years?"

Bess snorted. "Your father is a professional man. Delly Harper couldn't tie his own shoes without a map and a flashlight."

"Hey, that's just mean," said the ghost in question. "She has a prune pit where her heart should be and a sour lemon stuck up her butt."

I'd never heard Delly utter a word against anyone before, and I sort of agreed with him, which made it difficult to hold back a smile.

Since Bess couldn't hear Delly, she only shut up because Martha flapped a hand at her.

"Enough of airing your many opinions that we don't have time to listen to. The hunt will last less than a week now that we lost a day to rain. We think the best way to capitalize on the opportunity is to divide the town into sections where people can come and cheer on each team."

Hands clasped earnestly in front of her ample bosom, Patricia twittered, "We're using the colored banners from the spring fling." She'd have said more, but Martha clapped her hands for silence.

"You'll be quite proud," she said, "of the way we've got the ball rolling already."

I let myself be settled into a chair around the planning table—mostly because my knees went weak with trepidation. "What ball rolling?"

"Well, we couldn't afford to wait around while you were off doing whatever it is you do when you're not helping, now could we?"

You mean living my life? I thought but didn't say.

"Since time was of the essence, we've already issued the press release and posted the schedule of events on the town website and social media pages just like you taught us."

Regret. That was what I was feeling—so much regret for allowing them to see into my bag of tricks.

"We've only heard back from three food truck owners so far, but we can always get the locals to set up booths to take up the slack, so that's the food mostly handled."

"And the plastic outhouses," Bess chimed in. "I took care of those."

Patricia tapped the list clamped to a clipboard. "I got in touch with the usual artists and craftsmen, and even with short notice, it looks like we'll have a decent turnout."

Some of the regret gave way to a sense of pride at the way they'd pulled together the bare bones of an event in almost no time. Maybe there would come a time when they could handle things without me.

Today would not be that day.

"Looks like my work here is done, then. You ladies did a fine job without any help from me. You should be proud of your good work. Now, if you'll excuse me, I've—"

Martha rolled right over me. "All that's missing is the entertainment, and that's where you come in. The theme," she said, pausing for dramatic effect, "is mining. Now, get out your phone and drum us up something wonderful to keep the kiddies occupied while the mommies and daddies shop."

There are times when Martha reminds me of a demented clown. This was one of them.

"It's a phone, Martha, not a magic wand. Mining isn't exactly a popular party theme. What do you expect me to do? Have a truckload of sand hauled in so kids can dig up their own buried treasure?"

I, of course, meant that as a joke. Martha thought the idea had merit and hounded me until I made the calls to put it in place, though on a somewhat smaller scale than she wanted. We went with a dozen large, plastic kiddie pools to keep the mess at least partially contained, and then I played a rousing game of phone tag to find a supplier of polished gemstones to make up the treasure.

During my online search, I turned up a small business in the western part of the state that offered kids a mobile mining experience. For a slightly higher than reasonable sum—because of the short notice— the company would set up a tent with a gemstone sluice and geode cracking stations. We'd charge admission to cover the costs and maybe eke out a little profit.

Patricia got so excited, Bess yelled at her to stop bouncing before she fell and broke a hip. That started off a waged war between them, and I managed to slip out as Martha waded in to break it up.

# CHAPTER EIGHT

The Mooselick Treasure Hunters Association—I kid you not, that is what they decided to call themselves—held their first meet and seek on the Tuesday following Delly's funeral. It did not start out well.

First, there was a disagreement about how many helpers each man was allowed to bring. The agreed-upon number had been one, but Harley Stanfield's wife had to work extra hours all week so he could take time off, which meant he had to bring both his boys along. Able Gallow—who had a brother named Willing, by the way—allowed how he had two brothers-in-law but only invited one. If he'd known it was okay to play fast and loose with the rules, he'd have done something different.

The brother-in-law in question stood out from the rest by way of being a bit overdressed for the occasion—at least compared to Able and Harley, who both looked like they'd done a day's hard work already. In tan slacks and a short-sleeved button-down, Bill Cavanaugh looked exactly like what he was, a banker out of his element.

"Geez Louise, Able," Harley waved an arm around to emphasize his annoyance. "It ain't like my youngest is a digging fiend or anything. He's only seven years old. Caroline's coming to pick them up around noon, and she's already pissed off at me. Give me a break."

Able's face darkened up like a thundercloud, and my dad had to step in to smooth things over before the discussion turned ugly. With the first hurdle past, he drew the men's attention to the aerial map he'd cajoled my mother into using the library's thirty-six-inch printer to make and then mounted on a foam core presentation board.

"I pulled this footage off one of those satellite maps on the Internet. This," he said, pointing to a blue line that ran in a square shape around the center of the map with one side angled to account for the Barrow's Quarry trench, "is the border of the property."

Next, he pulled a folded sheet of paper out of his pocket. "According to Delly, Clint left these instructions: From the tree we planted for my mother, walk one hundred and fifty paces toward the marker where we buried Shep."

Harley finally broke the dead silence that followed. "Who the hell was Shep?"

Give the man a nickel for asking the question of the day.

"I'm assuming a beloved dog, or maybe a horse. I came out yesterday in the rain to take a look around and found a roughly drawn map on the inside of the shed door. Delly marked all of his dig sites and crossed off places he didn't think were viable sites. Helpful since we have a general idea where he's been and where not to go. I've transferred his marks to this map."

I made a mental note to visit the map in the shed before I left for the day.

Pointing to a circled area left of the center of the map, dad continued in his best teacher's voice, "This is where it looks like Delly concentrated his efforts. You'll see that when we head over there. We're starting where he finished because it feels like the right thing to do. Anything we find, as per his wishes, gets divided among us. My share, should there be one, will go toward any final expenses not covered by the benefit dinner."

"Do you really expect to find anything buried out here?" Bill Cavanaugh spoke for the first time.

My dad grinned. "No, but we're here to honor Delly's final request, so let's get down to it."

"Jes—" Glancing at his sons, Harley broke off before he said a cuss word they'd repeat to his wife. "Jiminy Christmas! A man could spend a lifetime out here poking holes in the ground based off those instructions."

A man basically had.

"Does it say how deep to dig?"

"Are all the jars buried in one spot?"

Thick and fast, the questions came, and my father had the same answer for all of them. Delly hadn't left anything other than Clint's instructions.

Harley exhibited a hand curled into a fist. "You mean to tell me we're hunting for seven jars smaller than this, and all we have to go on for landmarks are trees and some sort of marker that we don't know what it is? My wife was right. This is not worth listening to her complain about working all the extra hours for a week. I'm out of here. C'mon boys, let's pack it up."

"Wait." My dad held up a hand to stop the exodus. "Just hold on a minute. I'd rather not spend any more time than necessary, either, so I thought we might save some time with this." He reached through the passenger's window and pulled out a metal detector.

Everyone went quiet for a moment, then Harley said, "We really are doing this, aren't we? I almost don't want to find anything, you know?"

The notion sobered the rest of the men—other than Bill, who continued to look bored. "Delly didn't ask for help, or half the town would have pitched in," Able said. "Maybe that's his fault for being a stubborn fool who poked into other people's business to see if he could help and always gave more than he got. I tried to do the best I could by him. I suppose him being dead is no reason to stop now."

With his round, sunburned face, his green cap, and faded overalls, no one would have taken Able for being a deep or insightful thinker. His comment proved that theory wrong.

"This is our last chance to do something for Delly. Let's make him proud and if there's anything to find, give it our best shot in his memory." And on that note, my dad handed me the metal detector, showed me how to use it, and the hunt for buried treasure began in earnest.

Mostly quiet, we hiked around the house past an area that looked like it had once been a lovely garden but now held only some overgrown rose bushes and some purple and white lilacs, their flowers almost fully faded. A moldering length of old rope hung from a thick branch of an old oak. Probably the remnant of an old tire swing.

If I'd thought the house felt lonely and sad from the inside, the backyard intensified those feelings to the point I had to shrug them off as I followed my father toward the towering maple standing in the center of the cleared field behind. Some fair distance out from it, we had to step over a set of stones in a concentric circle around the tree. Then another, and finally, a third ring.

The field stretched out wide, the stones looking oddly alien in their perfect placement as if the fairies had designated the maple home and designed for it a protective barrier. It took a moment for me to realize the stones represented years of Delly's life, and each one covered a place where he had looked for buried gold.

Hundreds of them.

"Doesn't look like Delly knew where to find Shep's marker, so he searched in every direction,"

Harley said what we all were thinking. "That's either genius or madness."

The next few minutes were taken up by each man beginning with his back against the tree and pacing out the required distance. No two men stopped in the same spot. The one who went the farthest ended up beyond the outermost ring of stones while the man with the shortest legs stopped before he got to the inner.

"This doesn't make sense to me at all," Harley's voice sounded loud. "If he thought the gold was over this way, what was Delly doing over on the other end of the property? There isn't even a good line of sight from here to the quarry's edge."

"Seems like after he'd gone all the way around, he probably decided this wasn't the right tree." An explanation that wasn't much of a stretch and also fit what Delly had said to me.

After a few minutes of discussion, the men decided we'd spend the morning ruling out the mighty maple's perimeter and then move on to rule out another area where Delly had dug.

The quarry precipice fell into one of Delly's crossed out areas, and I got the impression none of the men were upset they wouldn't be forced to confront the painful spot where he had gone over the edge. I didn't blame them a bit.

Some metal detectors buzz, some whistle, this one made a sound somewhere in between. In the first ten minutes, we all learned to rate the find's depth based on the tone the machine made. By the end of the first hour, I learned I needed to work on toning my arms and shoulders. The swinging motion already made them pinch and promised to make me even sorer by the end of the day, but I'd covered a good chunk of the circle in that time and developed a system.

Harley's boys trailed behind me with a handful of marker flags. Whenever the detector buzzed, one of them would jam a flag into the ground to mark the spot where men should dig. We had two colors, yellow for when we heard the deeper tones and red for things that sounded closer to the surface.

"This is more fun than I thought it would be," Harley's eldest said, his brown eyes sparkling through a flop of dark hair. "Any chance I could get a turn with that?"

When we stopped for a break, and I turned to assess our progress. We were ahead of the men by a good twenty flags and had nearly completed a three-foot-wide swath around the outer perimeter. Now was as good a time as any for him to have a turn, and my shoulder could use the break.

"Sure. Just tell me when your arm tires out. That thing gets heavier as you go along." I showed him how to work the controls, and off he went with a mile-wide grin on his face.

Our second pass would cover the area between the stone rings, and the last, another three feet beside the inner.

"Can it read what's under these stones?" Harley's boy, who I guess was also named Harley since his father called him Junior. "Or is that a waste of time?"

What if we found the gold in a spot where Delly had already been digging? I'd feel horrible for him— more than I already did.

"I think we probably should. Just in case Delly missed something."

Some of the joy fell off Junior's face. "That's sad. I liked Delly. He was nice to me, and he always carried around this jar of stuff he found out here. He'd let us pick out things if we wanted to."

"Yeah," the younger brother chimed in, his eyes wide and serious. "I got a mustard ball."

"You idiot," Junior corrected. "You got a musket ball, not a mustard ball."

"Same thing."

"Is not."

"Is, too.

"Okay, well, why don't you tell me what else he had in the jar?" Anything to break up the argument. "What did you get, Junior?"

"I got a genuine arrowhead." He pronounced it gen-u-wine like Delly would have done. "And some foolish gold."

"That's fool's gold." The younger brother perfectly mocked the corrective tone of the elder. "See, you don't know everything. You only think you do."

Junior tossed his brother a quelling look. "I know more than you." He turned to me, "You wanna see what kind of stuff Delly found, you just need to look behind the seat of his truck. That's where he kept the jar."

Color me curious, but as we turned back to the job at hand, I made a note to find the jar. Junior managed another ten minutes before he handed the detector off to his little brother, who had announced he, too, wanted a turn. He didn't last long against the machine's weight before he handed it back, and I suggested the boys go look for Shep's marker.

"Ma'am," said the younger, his face grave with the effort to be respectful, but since when had I become a ma'am? "Do you have a plastic detector we can use? To find the marker, I mean." He looked at his brother. "Magic markers are made from plastic, right?"

My lips twitched with the effort not to smile. "They are, but Shep's is a different kind of marker. One that's used to mark a spot, not to draw with, so it's probably made of stone, or metal, or even wood. Maybe with writing on it."

"Yeah, don't be so stupid," Junior put up a credible sneer.

"You didn't know, either." The little guy wasn't having it.

Did toos and did nots drifted back until they passed out of my hearing range, leaving me alone with both detector and flags.

Well, with detector, flags, and Delly, who showed up as soon as the boys passed out of hearing range. Until the energy of his annoyance prickled across my skin, I was kind of enjoying the chill he brought to the rising summer heat.

"That's cheating." He pointed to the beeping machine. "You're a cheating cheater."

The buzz of his fury didn't create the headache that flared between my eyes, but it didn't do anything to lessen the pain, either.

"I'm sorry you feel that way," I hissed even though no one was close enough to hear me. "But we only have a few days before tax books close, and there's no money to pay them. We're in a hurry, and this was the fastest method we could find."

Delly blew out of there, leaving a vibration in the air that set my teeth on edge. On the one hand, it might have been helpful to have him around as a source of information. On the other, with him gone, he wouldn't be talking in my ear every minute of the day.

By the time Harley's wife showed up to pick up the kids, I'd covered nearly the entire circle. My gut refused to so much as flutter—a sign I took to mean we'd struck out.

"Almost done," I said to my father when he and Bill the banker joined me. "Find anything good?"

"Three dollars and seventy-six cents in change, a few bottle caps, and two old keys." Dad grinned and pulled me in for a one-armed hug. "I think it would be a good idea if you could go back and just double-check where we've been—we left the flags up for you —to make sure we didn't miss anything."

"Sure. I'll do that right after I finish up here." I rolled my sore shoulders and tried not to sigh over the extra work.

"It's going faster than I expected," Bill wiped some sweat off his brow with a snow-white hankie he'd pulled out of the pocket of his still-spotless pants. Looking at him, I couldn't figure what leverage Harley might have used to get him out here because digging in the dirt clearly wasn't a thing he did often enough to warrant purchasing the proper attire for the job.

Since I was here with an ulterior motive, I pried. "Did you know Delly well?"

"Me?" He looked surprised. "Hardly at all. My sister made me come."

When I cocked an eyebrow at him, he declared himself parched—his word, not mine—and volunteered to go back to where we'd left the cooler by the cars and fetch bottles of water for everyone.

"At the rate we're moving," my father speculated once we were alone again, "we should be able to finish ruling out all the previous dig sites by the end of the day tomorrow."

"If we don't find anything," Able walked over to join us. He eyed the metal detector with disdain, "then what?"

"Then, I guess we try to guess which tree might have been planted for Clint's mother and see if we can track down Shep's marker." Dad leaned on his shovel. "Or we could rent more detectors and canvass the entire property. I'm open, Able, to any suggestion you might have."

With the exception of my father, who wasn't on the schedule to teach summer classes this year, all of the men had jobs. We had four days left before the tax books closed—about two days more than I wanted to spend swinging a metal detector. But I hadn't come here for gold; I came to look for clues and solve a murder.

"Either way works for me," I chimed in with my opinion and hoped my shoulder and arm would hold out. If we went with the multi-detector method, Delly would have to deal with his disappointment, and I would have to speed up my efforts to pry information out of his friends.

"Delly would have loved this, you know." Harley had joined us in time to catch the end of the conversation. "All of us working together to find Clint's stash. I feel like we let him down by not helping more. I guess I had no idea how easy it would have been with the right equipment."

"You didn't know Delly at all, then." Able's eyes narrowed. "He'd have had a kitten with a cottontail if he was here right now. Old school, all the way. That was Delly right down to the ground. This high-tech stuff, he'd have called it a cheat, and I agree. One thing me and Delly had in common," he practically growled, "is our opinion on cheating. Any man who cheats is a man who won't blink an eye at lying or stealing. Such a man ain't worth spit."

Able had Delly's outlook on metal detectors pegged, and because he did, I bumped him to the top of my talking-to list.

"Now." To further emphasize his point, Able turned to spit a stream of tobacco out on the ground. "I don't believe there's so much as a single flake of gold buried out here. I also don't relish the idea of spending more'n a week pottering around with a pick and shovel to come up empty, so I'll go along with using that thing. I guess if you call it a tool, it ain't so much of a cheat, but I maintain Delly wouldn't like it."

I think that was the second-longest string of sentences I'd ever heard the man utter. Not that I'd spent any amount of time around him, but if I had to come up with one word to describe him, taciturn would be the one I'd have chosen.

"Maybe not," my dad clapped Able on the back. "Delly was a good man with a forgiving heart, and if I failed him in life by considering his passion a thing of fantasy, all I can do now is to see it through for him."

"Aw shucks. I guess I never thought of it like that." I heard Delly speak from somewhere behind me. Far enough back, he hadn't tripped my ghost sensing trigger. "How's a man supposed to keep up a full head of steam when his friends say such nice things?"

All I could do was shrug. Talking to ghosts in public is a good way to earn yourself a vacation in one of those nice hospitals where they let you wear the jackets with sleeves that tie in the back.

However, once I'd decided to talk to Able, getting a chance proved harder than expected. I kept on detecting while I waited for the right moment, but he stuck close to the others for the rest of the day.

When I finished way ahead of the men, I took a moment to wander over and inspect the place where Delly had fallen. If there'd been anything to see, and according to Ernie, there hadn't, a day of rain had washed the evidence away. All I could do was stand there and consider the possibilities.

When something was right on the surface, the metal detector warned me in the voice of an angry, robotic cat. *Weouw, weouw.* Since I'd forgotten to turn it off, I jumped when it went off as I was heading back from the edge of the quarry.

Out of reflex, I reached for a flag, then realized I didn't need one when the glint of metal shone out from between blades of grass. Silver, not gold, so nothing to do with Delly's quest, but I reached down to retrieve the object anyway and came up with a pretty, drop-style earring.

Nice piece, I assessed. Fine workmanship, made from quality metal, and the stone set in the center looked real. Not something I'd expect to see in this particular place, but for all I knew, Delly had a parade of women up here all the time. Unlikely, but possible.

He didn't seem the kiss and tell type, so who would ever know?

"Everly!"

When my father called me over to tell me I could leave for the day, I dropped the earring in my pocket and promptly forgot all about it.

CHAPTER NINE

The scents of lemon furniture polish and old books reached out and drew me in as they always did when I stepped inside the town library. I'd practically grown up tucked into one comfy nook among the shelves or another, reading or playing with my Barbie dolls while my mother tended to the books and the patrons who borrowed them.

She and I have had our moments of unrest, but reading was always our common ground. We could fight for an hour, then discuss our latest read over dinner without missing a beat. It worked for us.

I found her in her office sorting through a box of books waiting for repair or restoration—a task she approached with the same assessing nature as a triage nurse tending to patients in an emergency room. When she saw me, she pulled off the magnifiers she used for fine work and blinked until her eyes refocused.

"Anything good come in?" If there was one thing my mother loved, it was a book so damaged it challenged all of her skills. She doesn't like to toot her own horn, but she's been called on to do restoration work for the Smithsonian more than once.

"First edition of The Pothunters."

"What's it need?"

"A fair bit. The binding's cracked, the papers and boards are a mess." Her eyes gleamed with anticipation. "I can't wait to dig in. Are you looking for something new to read? I have recommendations."

"Not today," I said. "Today, I'm in research mode."

"My favorite mode. What's the topic?"

Since it seemed less than prudent to admit I wanted to dig up dirt on Delly's family, I used a different point of reference. "Point me in the direction of everything you have on the Marlow."

I'd stopped in at home to shower and take Molly for a romp but still had plenty of time to scan through microfilm of old newspaper archives. It came as a surprise when my mother sat down at her computer instead of heading toward the corner where the microfiche machine rested under a tan cover with green piping.

A few taps of the keys brought up a program I hadn't seen her use before.

"I applied for a grant and used the money to buy the library a large-format scanner. Then I asked some of the volunteers to help with digitizing old newspaper editions and other documents we have on file."

"That sounds...tedious, but interesting."

Mom's eyes lit up. "Oh, it has been. Once we got the bulk of the newsprint scanned, we ran the resulting images through an OCR program to translate them into search capable text." She moved aside and gestured for me to take her place. "It was a nightmare until we updated the Optical Character Recognition software and then had one of your father's colleagues come in and help us figure out the best settings. He whipped up a nifty little program and workflow to catch the more common errors and refine the process."

Reaching over my shoulder, she one-finger typed Marlow Inn into the search box. The hands on a clock icon circled while the results tabulated.

"You should have seen the gobbledygook that first version put out. It would have taken less time to hand type every article than to fix the thousands of errors. I thought I would have to apologize to the board for making a huge mistake with the purchase, but now we've got a working system, and it's a boon to be able to search the archives. We still come across some garbled text once in a while, but most of the bugs seem to be out of the system.

When the list finally scrolled down, it was longer than I expected.

"I think the board is lucky they hired you. It would have taken hours to scan through the stacks for even half the information I now have at my fingertips. You really outdid yourself with this one."

"Oh, go on." Her face tinged ever so slightly pink. My mother went into self-deprecation mode and waved off the compliment. "Anyone would have done the same."

"No, they wouldn't. This is a very good thing, and I'm proud of you."

She went back to her work, and I dug into the information so helpfully spread before me, taking notes about the inn and about Delly's family as I went along. The library volunteers had been busy because not only had they scanned in old newspapers, they had also added the town reports to the mix.

When I'd finished the initial search, I went

ahead and keyed in another search for the name Clint Jackson and followed the trail of information down through to Delly and Carlene. Or mostly to Carlene because Delly didn't pop up much. I found him in the obituaries of his parents, then featured in an article explaining how he'd saved a puppy from a burning building, and finally in the public notices when he lost the inn for non-payment of taxes.

After losing his parents within a year of each other, Delly tried to keep the inn going. He even managed to for a couple of years. Then, according to what I could piece together from his comments, the town reports, and the notice of foreclosure in the paper, he'd been unable to pay the mortgage.

Sadly, even if he'd kept it another couple of years, the funneling of tourism toward Hackinaw would have put him in the same situation. A worry that David might soon face, but then, Delly hadn't had me or the force of Martha behind him. Just one more time when he gave more than he got.

If I hadn't attended his funeral, I'd have thought Delly to be exactly what he'd looked like: a funny character of a man with few means who indulged in the odd hobby of digging around for a possibly false legend. I'd have been wrong. Delly was a hero in his own way.

I hovered the mouse over Clint's name, but sheer curiosity led me to click on the first of several links to information on Carlene Nicholson instead. Something about her—no, everything about her— just flat ticked me off and because it did, set off alarm bells in my head.

There didn't seem to be any reason for her to kill her step-cousin, but I wanted her to be guilty because she'd been mean to me, and I just didn't like her. Petty of me, and yet, the nagging finger-pointer in my head did a happy dance and refused my efforts to shake her off. So I dug in to look at the first link, though technically, it wasn't about Carlene at all. Or at least I didn't think it was.

"Hey, Mom. I think your new and improved process missed this one, and you're right; the text looks like it was written mostly in gibberish. Who's this?" I indicated the photo that came along with the article. It featured a blonde woman who looked like she'd just stepped down off a pageant stage with every blonde hair and every fold of her stylish, red dress perfectly arranged.

Sighing, my mother returned to stand behind me.

"Ah, I'd forgotten all about her. That's Grace Belanger."

"Doesn't ring a bell."

"No." Mom leaned around me to take control of the mouse and run the article through whatever program it was that would translate it into being readable. "You weren't visiting much at the time, and she didn't stick around long. Made quite a splash while she was here, though."

I glanced at the computer to see that the fixing of the file would take a few minutes. I didn't want to wait that long to read the story. "Why don't you tell me about her?"

"There's not much to tell. She blew into town when real estate sales started to come back after the crash. Granted, we're a little behind the times here in Mooselick River, so the rest of the country had already begun to level off a few months earlier. I think that's probably what drew her here."

I tapped my fingernails on the table while calculating the dates. "That would have been just before the whole restoration of Hackinaw fired up. Am I right?"

Mom nodded her head toward the computer. "She had a hand in that, actually, and made a lot of promises about how the revitalization project would have a trickle-down effect for Mooselick River. Well, I guess we all know how that went."

If the state hadn't decided to bypass our town with a new, faster route to the resort area, the plan might have worked. Instead, Mooselick River hadn't fared well until I'd come back to town and helped a band of determined women find ways to draw tourists off the beaten path. We'd had some misses, but also some hits, and slowly, we were making progress.

"So basically, her name is mud around here."

"Worse than," Mom agreed. "When anyone talks about her at all. You see, we all figured she knew what was coming since she sneaked out of town the same night we threw a banquet in her honor. That article came out on the morning after, right next to the state's announcement about the new road system and how it would give Hackinaw a huge boost by speeding up access to the area. When a group of concerned citizens went to talk to Grace about what to do to stop it from happening, she was already gone. Lock, stock, and barrel. That's when we figured we'd been had."

With the exception of some of my fashion choices

in high school and her utter disdain for the man I'd married, my mother isn't particularly critical of others. She'd been proved right in her instincts about Paul, I had to admit, though I stood by my low-rise jeans and tied-at-the-waist flannel shirts. Still, she hadn't thrown her victory back in my face, which had gone a long way toward making our relationship better, but there was vitriol in her tone when it came to Grace.

"Once everyone started talking, we learned she was the one who put together the land deals and made herself a hefty profit. Plus, there was speculation she got some kind of kickback from the state. All we know is the backstabber left town before anyone could confront her, and she hasn't been seen since."

Interesting, but probably not pertinent to my current investigation unless...

"How does Carlene Nicholson tie in with all of this? Her name was mentioned somewhere in there, too."

"Carlene worked for Grace. Office manager or something. I think she was planning to go for her Real Estate license, but I could be wrong because she never did."

"And no one asked her about what happened after Grace left town?"

"Most likely, but I'm sure I'd have heard if she'd said anything worth knowing. Maryann Payne took over, and the first thing she did was let Carlene go, but the land deals held, and the road went in, and the rest is history."

My phone beeped to signal a reminder. "Whoops, I lost track of time. I got sidetracked this morning, and I still need to drop off the lease for Tulip. Is there any way you could send me that article once the text is all fixed?"

I got a patented Kitty Dupree eye-roll. "Don't you ever visit the library's website? I swear I don't know why I bother sometimes. There's a link to the digitized archives in the left sidebar."

"Well, how was I supposed to know what digitized archives meant?"

"Oh, I don't know. Maybe from the big information banner on the front page."

It's humbling when your mother has better technical skills than you do.

And annoying when she rubs it in.

# CHAPTER TEN

"What is up with you?" Jacy thrust a squirming bundle of baby into my arms, and I lost track of her question as little Wade charmed me with a toothless grin and then twined chubby fingers into my hair.

Because they were there and looked so juicy and sweet, I kissed his little cheeks and babbled at him.

"Who's a little cutie? I'm gonna kiss those smoochie-cheeks. I'm gonna kiss them right now."

Wade rewarded my efforts with a giggle that melted my already gooey heart. What can I say? The child was adorable, and he smelled really good, too—sort of powdery and new.

"You can talk baby talk to my son all day, but you're not getting out of answering the question."

It seemed like a bad idea to tell Jacy her stern face looked just like her mother's.

"Nothing's up." But I couldn't look her in the eye.

"Don't tell me nothing's up. Aren't you supposed to be at kick-butt boxing class with lover boy tonight instead of inviting Peanut and me over to scarf down takeout lasagna?"

"I'm a grown-up; I can be where I want to be. So I skipped a session." I settled the baby on my hip, winced at the way the muscles pinched even after a hot shower and generous application of liniment.

Jacy knew about my past hauntings, but I hadn't told her about Delly yet, and I wanted to keep it that way because she'd insist on trying to help. My record for putting ghosts to rest by dealing with their killers included getting myself into some dangerous spots. After almost getting Jacy killed, too, I refused to drag her down with me if anything like that happened again. She had a family to think of now, so putting her in danger was off the to-do list entirely.

With an economy of movement, Jacy pulled off the detachable seat and left the stroller on the porch. Once inside the door, she set the seat on the floor, popped both hands on her hips, and stared at me. Or more accurately, into me.

"Don't try to fool me, Everly Dupree. I know you, and I can tell when something's up." It didn't take her long to put things together and come to the right conclusion. "You're acting weird, and someone's dead. Delly Harper didn't just fall off a cliff, did he?" She had the crazy eyes as she scanned the hallway for signs of the ghost. "Is he here right now?"

I'm a lousy liar, to begin with, and Jacy knows me better than anyone except my mother, but I gave it a shot anyway.

"Ernie didn't find any evidence of murder." There, I thought, a chance to mislead while still telling an utter truth.

Jacy didn't buy a word of it.

"Hah," she scoffed. "I like Ernie Polk as much as the next person, and we both know he does the best he can, but if there's a ghost in the house, it means our esteemed cop missed a vital piece of evidence. It would not be the first time."

"Fine." I caved. "Somebody murdered Delly Harper. Are you happy now?"

"Of course, I'm not. I liked the man. Who would want to kill him, though? Other than a penchant for talking a person to death, he was harmless. It doesn't make sense. What does he have to say for himself? Is he here now?" Her head swiveled again.

"I have no idea," I answered her questions in the order she asked them. "Not much, and no, he's not here at the moment. You would be able to tell because my eyes would be completely glazed over."

Rife speculation lit Jacy's as she pursed her lips. "Don't you always say most murders happen because of love, money, jealousy, or revenge? It's sad, but I don't think Delly had anyone, do you?"

"He had Pearl, but I doubt his cat had anything to do with the motive."

Head tilted sideways, Jacy gave me a look.

"Fine, I'll concede the possibility given we were nearly killed over my dog, but really, what are the odds of us getting caught up in a second pet-related murder?"

With his little fists still wrapped in my hair, Wade gave a pretty good imitation of his mother's derisive snort. I couldn't help but smile as I carried him into the living room, settled on the sofa, and put my feet up on the coffee table so I could rest the baby on my bent knees.

"And really," I said. "Should we be talking about such dire subjects in front of the baby?"

Jacy's eyes narrowed.

"As long as you talk like this," she infused the words with fake cheer while wearing a smile that came off as a half-grimace and, compared to her tone, frankly, creeped me out a little. "He won't have a clue we're talking about murder or the ghostly things that go bump in the night."

Way to shoot down my objections.

"Whatever, Jace." I gazed down at the baby and thought he looked too wise to be fooled. But then, because it was right there and because doing so always made him giggle, I buried my face in his belly and made babbling noises. He rewarded me by grabbing my hair again and yanking my head down so he could bite my nose with his toothless gums, which made me giggle along with him.

"Delly," I continued once the nose biting turned into signs of hunger, and I'd handed the baby off to his mother for feeding. "Doesn't go bump in the night."

While Jacy tucked pillows under her arm to help hold the baby's weight, I went to the kitchen for iced herbal tea. When I returned, she squinted and tilted her head.

"You know, Delly was a fixture here in town, but I can't recall anyone ever saying a word against him."

It was my turn to snort as I handed Jacy her tea.

"Still, it's possible he got on someone's bad side. He tells the most outrageous...," I paused to pick the right word, and lies seemed too strong because when Delly spoke of anyone, it seemed he believed he spoke the truth. "Stories about people. He doesn't seem too concerned about being dead, either."

"He was one of those guys you see around all the time, and because you see them, you think you somehow know them. Like I never would have pegged Delly as the type of person to have any sort of dark history. I always kind of figured he was a *what you see is what you get* type of man."

"Dark history?" I frowned.

"Well, he almost had to have one, didn't he?" Jacy sipped her tea, then handed the glass back to me so I could set it down on a coaster. "For someone to go to the trouble of pushing him off a cliff. No one does that unless it's personal."

"Except when something similar nearly happened to us last year, and it wasn't personal," I pointed out.

"Pfft." Jacy waggled her fingers at me dismissively. "Just because Christine Murray was so far off her rocker it wasn't even on the porch anymore doesn't mean attempting murder wasn't personal. Besides, she was going to kill us first and then push our bodies into the quarry. That's not the same."

Regardless of the semantics Jacy applied to the situation, she wasn't entirely off the mark. Whoever killed Delly, they had a reason. I just wasn't sure how to find out what it was after the fact, given I hardly knew the man. But Jacy was right about one thing, most murders came back to the same few motives: love, money, and revenge. Any other reason was just a subset of those three.

Once the food came and the baby went down for a nap, we discussed the possibilities over lasagna and salad.

"Why don't you just ask him what happened right before he died?" She waved her fork at me, then used it to spear a glistening cherry tomato half from her salad.

"Hah! That would be too easy," I sighed. "Then I could just feed Ernie the information and poof, ghost begone. It doesn't work like that."

Jacy leaned closer and turned one ear toward me as if to hear some juicy gossip. "How does it work?"

"Well," I tried to find the right words. "If a ghost thinks too hard about how they died, they have a...I guess the best term for it would be a fit. They shake until they blur, and make the air in the room feel like it's made of electricity." My throat tingled just thinking about it. "It's not pleasant."

Shock sent Jacy's fork rattling into the bowl when she dropped it. "Wait, you can feel the...whatever it is that happens?" Her eyes went wide, and she reached across to grab my hand. "Is it dangerous? Why didn't you tell me?"

"It's nothing, Jace. I promise." Rising, I gathered up the dirty dishes, put them in the dishwasher. "All it means is I can't ask Delly for details, and since, like you, I didn't have much to do with him in life, I'm left to parse out possible motives with almost no useful information to go on."

Basically, just another day with just another ghost.

Still, Jacy waited until I sat back down, and she could pin me with a look to see if I was fudging things to keep her from worrying. Finally satisfied, she tapped her fingertips on the table.

"Okay, then," she said. "What do we know about Delly Harper?" Then she jumped up. "Wait, we need to make notes." Because she'd helped me move into the house, she knew where to find a pad and a pen, which she licked the tip of before starting to write. I shuddered.

"Why do you do that? It's weird, and the ink must taste nasty."

"I dunno. My dad does it. I must have picked it up from him."

She wrote Delly's name on the top of the page and looked at me expectantly.

"All I really know is Delly fell off a cliff out behind the Jackson place where he'd been digging around for jars of buried gold. His ghost is haunting me, so his death probably wasn't an accident." I flipped my hands to show palms up. "That's it. I can't think of a single good reason why anyone would kill him. He seems harmless to me."

"Can you not?" Jacy cocked an eyebrow, drew a line under Delly's name, then one that traveled down the page. At the top of the left-hand pane, she wrote the word Motives and then added Suspects on the right.

Under the *Motives* heading, she started a list.

-Found the gold, and someone killed him
for it

-Cheated with someone's spouse, and they
waited years to take revenge
-Saw something he shouldn't
-Wrong place, wrong time
-Was blackmailing someone, and they'd
had enough
-Caught stealing something
-Jealous or spurned lover
-Screwed over a partner in crime
-Family squabble that ended badly
-Learned a secret so deep and dark
someone would kill to keep it quiet

Ten motives seemed enough of a list, but when Jacy went to add suspects to the other side of the page, she hesitated. "This is where it gets tricky. You need to ask Delly about his friends and family."

"He didn't have any family," I told her what I already knew. "And I spent the day with some of his closest friends. Didn't get so much as a tingle from either of them."

"Then you'll just have to get more information. Be glad you have Delly as a source."

I braced my elbows on the table, dropped my head into cradled hands. "Do you have any idea what you're asking me to do?" Even to me, my voice sounded muffled. "He'll talk me into a coma."

"Hey, you're the one he's haunting. I guess it all depends on how long you want to have him in your life."

A fair point. "I'll ask."

CHAPTER ELEVEN

Pearl sat in the kitchen doorway still as a statue except for the last inch of her tail, which she twitched while she eyed me with disdain. Across the room, Molly watched the cat, her body occasionally quivering with the effort to sit still. One claw in the face had been enough to deter the dog from making a second friendly overture.

"You're going to have to learn to get along eventually," I said. Pearl merely tipped her nose up higher in the cat equivalent of a sneer while Molly tilted her head and cocked an ear. Her face said she doubted I had the first clue what I was talking about. Clearly, my little pep talk missed the mark, so I tried again. "What do you say, hmm? Can't we try to be a happy family?"

Delicately, Pearl turned her head and yakked up her breakfast. I took that as a sign.

As I cleaned up the last of the mess, the doorbell rang. "Everly, it's me. I'm coming in." Patrea Heard used the key I'd given her back in the winter. "I've got news."

"Don't let the cat out," I called out as the door opened. Pearl had taken herself off somewhere, and for all I knew, she was sitting at the door waiting to escape.

"The what? Wait, when did you get a cat?" Dark hair swirled around an interesting face as Patrea looked for the cat. "Boy or girl? What breed?"

"The other day. Girl. And I have no idea. She's white with patches, and her name is Pearl."

Patrea bent to check under the table. "Where is she?"

"No idea. She hasn't decided if I'm friend or foe, so she hides behind the furniture and pounces on my feet a lot."

It still came as a slight shock to see my formerly buttoned-up attorney wearing jean shorts and a pink tee, her toenails painted to match. She'd loosened up a lot since her flu-enforced winter vacation in Mooselick River, and I didn't think falling in love was the only reason. I credited small-town living—even if it was only part of the time—with taking away some of the strain. Today, though, I noticed some faint frown lines around her eyes.

"Coffee or tea?"

"Coffee. And I have news." She followed me back to the kitchen, gave Molly a scratch behind one ear, then grabbed her favorite mug out of the cabinet above the coffeemaker.

"It's bad news." I didn't make it a question since three sugars, and a dose of cream in her coffee meant Patrea wasn't in the best of moods.

"Well, it's not good, but it could be worse." She sipped. She frowned. She set the cup down and slid it off to the side. "Paul's attorney petitioned the court to get his trial date moved up."

I sucked in a breath, held it for a moment as I processed the news, decided I wasn't as upset as I thought I'd be, and then let it out. "When?"

"Next Tuesday."

Luck smiled on me—and believe me, I later learned precisely to what extent—the day I discovered my ex cheating with my neighbor and former friend. As if one betrayal wasn't quite enough to take me down, the new lovebirds tried to frame me for embezzling funds from my in-law's charitable foundation. When that effort failed, Reva followed it up by trying to kill me.

There was no love lost between Paul and me, and

I assumed he wasn't done being a pain in my butt because I could see Patrea holding the other shoe in perfect drop position.

"And?" I prodded.

"You need to be there," Patrea's mouth firmed into a thin line as I poured myself another cup.

"Goes without saying." Pearl chose that moment to tear through the kitchen with all the grace of a stampeding herd. One spectacular leap gained her the table, scattered the sugar bowl, and shoved Patrea's mug perilously close to the edge.

"Eek," Patrea said, and then, "Aw, what a cutie."

I quirked an eyebrow. "How could you tell? All I saw was a white blur." Then a thought occurred. "Why don't you take her?"

Delly wouldn't mind—I hoped—and besides, what could he do? Haunt me harder? Other than the incessant chatter, I'd found him harmless so far.

But Patrea shook her head. "I can't for...well, there are reasons. We'll talk about them when there's not an ordeal hanging over your head."

"That sounds ominous. What ordeal? Just tell me. I can't bear the suspense."

Patrea's cup clicked down on the table hard enough to make Molly jump. "You're on the list of witnesses for the prosecution. I expect you'll be served with a subpoena today."

Okay, that one came as something of a surprise. "The prosecution?" My mouth dropped open. "They want me to testify against Paul? I can't possibly imagine what they think I could tell them that would help their case."

Patrea nodded. "The prosecution isn't your biggest problem. The Hastings family spared no expense when they hired Colin Peterson to represent their sleezeweasel of a son. He's a shark, and he'll use whatever and whoever he can find to get a client off the hook. His go-to move is to use any means possible to discredit witnesses."

I wasn't sure what I ought to feel, but amusement probably shouldn't have hit the top of the list.

"It's not funny," Patrea insisted. "He'll do anything he can to get your testimony thrown out of court, and that includes going after your family. If you have any skeletons in your collective closets, you'd better tell me about them now."

Did seeing dead people count as skeletons? "Only weird thing in my closet was a pile of mannequin heads, and they weren't even mine. Let him come at me. I have nothing to hide."

Before she got up for a refill, Patrea rolled her eyes. "Everyone has something to hide even if it's nothing more than an embarrassing childhood incident. You must have one of those in your past, and if you do, he'll find it and twist it to put you in the worst possible light." She sounded worried.

Of course, I'd done some foolish things in my day, but I didn't see how any of them could come back to haunt me now. "There's nothing to worry about."

"Oh, really?" This time Patrea only dumped a scant teaspoon of sugar in her coffee, a sure sign her mood had improved. She picked up the cup, sipped, and stared at me over the brim. "Ever stole a candy bar from the grocery store?"

I shook my head.

"Ever get caught necking in a parked car." Okay, that one I'd done, but that was before my relationship with Ernie Polk had undergone the change to its current status. In high school, I could flirt my way around him just fine, so all he'd done was send me home with a stern warning.

"Underage drinking?" Patrea pushed. "Wild college parties, maybe toke a little weed?"

Now I was getting nervous. "Okay, Jacy and I

might have sampled some of the bottles her mom kept under the sink when we were in junior high, but I never smoked anything." I shuddered. "Not my thing."

"But you could have, right?"

There's not a lot to do on a Friday night in most small towns in Maine, so yeah, I'd been to a few pit parties during high school. And yeah, some of the kids lit up. I'd had the chance even if I hadn't partaken. "I suppose so."

"Then you're guilty by proximity. All he needs to do is find one person who can place you at a party where there was booze or drugs. He'll convince the jury you were a juvenile delinquent who probably hasn't changed all that much over the years."

As if I didn't have enough reasons to despise my ex-husband. Having my reputation trashed in a court of law was just the cherry on top of the sundae served up at the crappy end to what I'd thought was a good marriage. That's what hurt the most, that I never saw it coming.

"What about the deposition I already made to say I didn't know anything about what Paul did or didn't do with the foundation's money? It's the truth, and that should be enough. Isn't that what you have to pledge when you testify? To speak the truth, the whole truth, and nothing but the truth?"

Based on the pitying look Patrea sent my way, I guessed she thought me naive, and maybe I was, but I didn't want to rehash my every possible transgression.

"Speaking of truth, do you think Paul told his parents how I found him? I bet he didn't, or they'd be eager not to have me testify at all."

Call me petty, but I still got a tickle out of the memory of my ex-husband naked and chained to a hotel bed by the tramp he'd dumped me for—the tramp that tried to kill me. That kind of comeuppance rarely ever happens.

Still, if I was counting my blessings, the end of my marriage certainly numbered high on the list. His attorney could rake me over the coals in court, but I was free of Paul, and no one could take that away from me.

"Keep that attitude," Patrea said when I expressed the sentiment. "You'll need it."

"Okay, enough with the depressing stuff. Tell me something good to balance it all out." I still had half an hour before I needed to leave for Delly's place and another day of swinging the metal detector. My shoulder issued a protest at the very thought.

The first smile I'd seen from her since she showed up played around Patrea's lips, but she shook her head. "I want to, but this is more like a girl's night piece of news. Do you think we could round up the usual suspects for Cappy's this week?"

I tried to pry it out of her, but she held firm until I ran out of time, so I promised to see if I could get the gang together.

## CHAPTER TWELVE

Day two of the treasure hunt went much like the first only my shoulder muscles registered their protest early and with great enthusiasm.

Offer to go treasure hunting, I said. It will be fun, I said. Right.

"Hey, Able. How's it going today?" I caught him away from the group and swung over near him for a double-check detection pass that was probably a complete waste of time.

Dirt and rocks flew as the shovel in his meaty hands rose and fell like a piston. The sun laid darker patches of red across his cheeks and the tip of his nose where the brim of his cap hadn't quite given enough shade.

"Hot."

"Seems like you knew Delly pretty well."

"Well enough, I s'pose." Ting went the shovel.

"Do you know if he was seeing anyone?"

Able gave me a look that I had no trouble reading. He didn't think Delly's love life or lack of same was any of my business.

"Why do you ask?"

"Oh, you know. We'll be packing up his things, and I thought maybe if he had a woman friend, some of her stuff might be at his place." My face went hot and probably redder than his, which was pretty red since he had declined my offer of sunscreen.

"Not that I ever heard. Delly kept that kind of thing to himself."

"But he dated sometimes, right?" I wanted the answer to be yes and not just because of the investigation into his death. The more I knew of Delly, the more I hated to think of him out here alone all the time.

Straightening up, Able took off his cap, pulled a bandanna out of his pocket, and used it to wipe sweat from his brow. "I dunno. Probably. He didn't throw himself off a cliff out of a broken heart if that's what you're asking."

I felt the burn from his look.

"No, I wasn't suggesting—"

"Good! Because I've heard what people are saying. It was an accident, that's all. Delly wouldn't do away with himself."

"That's not the only rumor flying around."

"No one would have hurt him, either. He was the salt of the earth. A good man who never cheated anyone out of so much as a nickel."

He slapped the cap back on his head and bent to apply shovel to hole again. I knew I'd been dismissed.

And I hadn't learned a single piece of useful information except that based on his reaction, Able didn't know anyone who had it out for Delly. But then, what had I expected? Only Delly's killer could fill in the blanks. Able's grief looked and felt genuine to me and not motivated by any more remorse than people normally feel when they lose someone.

"You couldn't have stopped what happened," I spoke to Able's back. "But wherever he is, I'm sure Delly knows you would have if you could. You know he'd want you to remember him for the way he lived and not the way he died. Keep telling those stories about him. That's how you'll keep him with you. Just remember him; that's all anyone can ask."

Able stopped shoveling for a moment. He never turned, never spoke, only nodded. Then the shovel fell again, and I moved on to find Harley and see what he had to say.

Less than Able, as it turned out. Harley hadn't seen Delly for a couple of weeks before he died, didn't have any idea whether a woman had ever set foot on the property, and by the way he smirked, didn't think much of the possibility.

Sometime after noon, I finished up with the last of the spots marked with an X on the map. I found it sobering to think that in two days, we'd covered all the same ground it had taken Delly years to check, and then some.

Tenacity, thy name was Delmar Harper.

"Hey, Dad, where do you want me now?"

"Well, we've had a talk about the next steps, and there's disagreement in the ranks. Harley thinks we should rent more metal detectors, and Able is in favor of picking the most likely tree and putting us through our paces, as it were."

Dad's hugs are awesome; his jokes are not.

"What do you think?"

"Logically, Harley's plan holds more water. We could divide the property into a grid, tackle each section methodically. But to be honest, this whole thing is more fun than I expected it to be. Don't tell your mother I said that, by the way." He grinned as I mimed zipping my lips. "What do you think?"

"I think," I looked back toward the house, "that if I wanted to plant a tree for mom, I'd probably choose the corner of the yard where she put in the rose-bushes after Grammie Dupree died." Thinking about memorializing my mother sent ice to whisper through my veins. "Somewhere close where I could see it every day, and maybe sit beneath the branches to think about her. I probably wouldn't plant it in some random location, but that's just me."

"Sounds like you think we're searching too far afield."

"I guess I do, but it's not my call. From what I can tell, it's you and Able against Harley. Where does Bill come down in the debate, and does he get a vote at all?"

"He's on Harley's side, or as he put it, he's in favor of expediency. Looks like you're the tiebreaker."

"Oh no, you're not dragging me into this. I'm just here to play with the metal detector."

Because fishing for information among Delly's friends hadn't panned out any better than looking for clues, which reminded me to ask, "Do you know if Delly had a lady friend?"

"A few years back, but not that I'd heard lately. Why do you ask?"

"Idle curiosity. Just wondering if he had someone special. Maybe someone who'd like to help pack up his things."

Dad sighed. "Afraid not. I've decided to leave that chore until this one is finished, and I can talk your mother into lending a hand."

"And by lending a hand, you mean taking one look at your feeble efforts and taking over the job herself." A tactic that fooled no one.

"She has her strengths," he agreed. "Why don't you call it a day. We'll spend another couple of hours clearing the last of those flags, and I'll do the final pass with the detector. Give me a chance to play with it awhile."

My shoulders nearly wept with gratitude.

"Okay if I make a pit stop at the house?" The men had no problem wandering off into the woods if they felt a need. I wasn't about to do the same. Plus, while I was in there, I could take a quick look around without Ernie or anyone else breathing down my neck.

"Go ahead."

I got one of his hugs on my way past and felt better for it.

Delly's house felt emptier than it had the day I'd picked up his cat until he popped up in the kitchen and began telling me stories about the furniture.

"Excuse me for one moment," I took off for the bathroom and the blessed silence. Delly was too much of a gentleman to talk to me through the door. I might have lingered a bit longer than necessary, and I might have also taken a quick tour of his medicine cabinet. You can learn a lot about a person that way.

What I learned about Delly is that he took medicine for his blood pressure but had otherwise been in decent health. The cabinet was bare of anything a woman might leave at the house of the man she was sleeping with. In fact, the shelves held little more than a razor, toothbrush and toothpaste, some hair cream that looked like it had been there for years, and a can of something called Bag Balm. That last was a product meant for use on a cow's udder. What Delly did with it, I didn't want to know.

Trying to be quiet so he wouldn't hear me, I checked all the drawers for a hairdryer or curling iron and came up empty there as well.

When I finally emerged, it was with no more

information than when I'd gone in, so I changed tack and got him talking about the gold.

"My dad assumes you never found Shep's marker, or else you'd probably have found the gold. Is he right?"

"Shep was Clint's dog. Big old German shepherd. There's a picture of him around here somewhere. Clint buried him somewhere on the property, but I never found anything that looked like a marker, so I never figured out where. My father didn't know, either. He and Clint fell out for a few years. Shep must have died during that time."

"Do you know why they argued?" Any more snooping would have to wait for another time. It felt too weird to peek in the closets with the ghost watching me. "Clint and your dad, I mean."

"Could have been all kinds of reasons. Clint wasn't an easy man to get along with from what my daddy told me. Ornery as a mule, and twice as stubborn is how he put it. Them two didn't speak to each other half the time, and toward the end, they even fought because Clint wouldn't come to stay at the inn so someone could be with him all the time."

He frowned at the memory. "My mother and father never fought much. Too much respect between them, but they had words over Clint, they did. I heard them arguing in the night. Didn't do no good, though. Clint wouldn't budge, and Daddy stayed out here for more than a week at the end even though it made my mother madder than a wet hornet."

"That must have been hard to hear. You said you were young, right?"

"Eleven. Daddy cried when Clint took his last breath. I'd never seen him cry before. Never did again, either."

How many times could my heart break for this man?

"Families are complicated. It sounds like your parents were good people, though." I offered the best comfort I could. "I'm sure they'll be waiting for you when you do go into the light."

"I hope so," he said. "I truly do." Overcome with emotion, he faded from sight.

After that, I didn't hang around long, but on the way out, I noticed Delly owned an answering machine, and on a hunch, I hit the play button.

*This is Harrison Blake from Blake, Blake, and Taft calling to discuss the offer on the piece of property bordering the quarry. Eli Barrow has agreed to meet your price. If you could call me back at your earliest conve-*

*nience, I can have papers ready to sign and a check for the amount by the end of the month.*

I played the message twice and wrote down the number. Finally. Some new information. I didn't know what it all meant, but it felt important.

And the next time I saw Delmar Harper, he had some explaining to do.

# CHAPTER THIRTEEN

"Everly, there's something I—" Right in the middle of what was supposed to be date night—one that had been delayed twice already—a man identifying himself as a reporter with the Bangor Daily News appeared next to the table where Drew and I were trying to eat dinner.

"Ms. Dupree, is it true the judge had to issue a subpoena to get you to testify on your ex-husband's behalf?"

I shook my head and looked at Drew with mute appeal. It only lasted a second, but I caught the tinge of annoyance in the way his eyes narrowed and the tightness around his mouth, though I didn't think either of those was directed at me. "Let's go," he said and tossed his napkin over a still-full plate.

"Ms. Dupree, did you refuse to testify?" The reporter's dark eyes darted from me to Drew and back again with no small amount of speculation. "Could you please answer the question?"

According to Patrea's orders, I was not supposed to engage with the press. I was supposed to remain cool, calm, and collected while giving them nothing to print or broadcast.

But Patrea wasn't there, and I wasn't cool, or calm, or collected. I was hungry, and the one bite of spaghetti and meatballs I'd managed to shovel into my mouth had been spectacular. I wanted more, and I wanted that more to come with some peace and quiet.

"Go away!" Naturally, I did not shout in the restaurant. "Leave me alone!"

Okay, maybe I did raise my voice. But only a little, and when the reporter pressed again, I might have leveled up.

"No, the defense didn't *have* to serve me a subpoena. The prosecution chose to do so. Most likely as a way to make me look bad...and isn't that why you're here? You don't really want to know the truth; you want a quote that you can slap on a headline to catch readers' attention. Something salacious because titillation sells more papers, doesn't it?"

It all came out in a rush that left me panting and put a wary look on the reporter's face. I couldn't remember what he'd said his name was, and I decided I didn't care.

"Now, get away from me before your headline ends up reading: Annoyed Ex-Socialite Shoves Meatball down Reporter's Pants!" To further make my point, I raised my chin, channeled my feisty grandmother, and threw him a venomous glare while Drew nearly choked on a snort. "We're done here."

While I stabbed my fork into a now-lukewarm meatball, Mr. Newspaper exited the restaurant amid a round of applause from the rest of the diners.

"I'm Everly Dupree, I'm the entertainment, and I'll be here all week," I muttered and decided the lowered temperature hadn't really hurt the flavor of the meal. "Where were we?"

A wry smile twisted Drew's lips. "I'm not sure I remember. Does this kind of thing happen often?" He put down his fork, picked up his wine glass, and sipped while I tried to decide if he truly wanted to know or if the question was a subtle criticism.

"What? Being accosted by the press while I'm eating or getting angry when being accosted by the press while I'm eating? One of those things leads quite naturally to the other."

If he was waiting for an apology for either, he

would be disappointed. I'm not a woman who indulges her temper very often, and in this case, I felt justified. "Though, if it's the former, I certainly hope not. I've had more than my share of fallout from my ex-husband's poor choices."

I didn't realize I'd been scrunching and squeezing my napkin until Drew's warm hand settled over mine and stopped the restless motion with a gentle caress.

"Take a minute to breathe, okay?" Still capturing my hand in his, Drew used the other to signal one of the staff to whom he spoke in a low tone. Whatever he said elicited a smiling response and the removal of our plates from the table. I watched mine go with regret. Apparently, the date was over. I pushed back my chair to get ready to leave.

"Not so fast," Drew motioned me back down. "We need to talk, and I'd prefer not to do this on an empty stomach, so I asked for our food to be reheated."

As if I could eat now that he'd uttered the four-word phrase that was the kiss of death for any relationship.

We. Need. To. Talk.

Translation: I'm dumping your butt. And forever ruining eating in your favorite restaurant again for you in the process. As all these negative thoughts raced through my head, I dropped my gaze to study a faint wine stain on the tablecloth. Tears threatened, and I knew if I looked at him, their promise would quickly become a reality.

The world narrowed to just the stain on the cloth and the litany in my head. I hadn't set out to get involved with someone again. Damn this man for exuding such a comforting presence that I'd let my guard down enough to start the slow slide before the big fall.

Losing him would hurt. More than I expected. More than I wanted.

The stain looked a little like Elvis.

It's funny how the mind twists and turns around a thing it doesn't want to look at too closely. I'd fallen farther than I thought when it came to Drew Parker.

Damn the man.

"Everly!" His voice penetrated, dragged my attention back to the present and the impending pain. "Eat something. I'm beginning to worry about you."

Steam wafted off the plate I hadn't even noticed had been set in front of me. I couldn't have taken a bite if my life depended on it. "Look, Drew, you're a nice man, and I know you're doing the best you can to make a difficult situation a little easier. Just get it over with, would you?"

And let me move on with my life.

Again.

I sat wooden while Drew shrugged and pulled a small metal shoe out of his pocket. He set the shoe in front of me with a flourish and waited for my response, which was slow to come.

"Well," he prompted after a moment of confused silence.

Who, in the history of ever, broke up with someone by giving them a Monopoly shoe? "I don't get it," I uttered the understatement of the decade.

"It's a shoe," he said.

"Yes, I can see that. What does it mean?"

His face tinged with pink. "I really blew this, didn't I? It means we've been seeing each other for several months, and I'd like us to take the next step." He gestured toward the shoe. "Shoe...step...I was trying to be clever. Guess I missed the mark."

My brain tried to change gears, but it took a moment to hit me that this was the opposite of being dumped.

"The next step?" I repeated like an idiot.

"Well, if I'm going to do this, I might as well go all

the way. Everly Dupree, I'd like to take the next step." Drew pulled out another token, the top hat. "And hang my hat," he added a green, plastic house. "At your place. I'm there more than at my place anyway, so I thought it might be time to make things official."

In the months since my last ghost, Amber, had gone into the light, I'd convinced myself the hauntings had been a mere interlude in my life. One that was over and done. After all, how many dead bodies does the average person find in a lifetime? I knew I'd made my quota and then some.

But then, Delly Harper had come along and flushed that notion down the proverbial toilet. How could I let Drew move in without telling him about my ghost problem? How was I supposed to pop the top on that jack-in-the-box? And once the clown was out and bouncing around on its spring, would Drew ever see me the same way?

Not likely, or else I'd have told him already.

That I hadn't before, and that I didn't want to now was a problem I wasn't sure I could solve. I didn't realize how long I'd gone without speaking until I caught sight of the look on Drew's face. I'd hurt him by not jumping on the idea with the enthusiasm he expected.

"Well, I guess I really stuck my foot in it." Drew picked up the shoe again and popped it back in his pocket. "Did you see what I did there?" Bless him for trying to lighten the mood, but I could feel the hurt rolling off him in waves.

"Drew, I'm sorry. You took me by surprise, and I've had a really weird day." The excuse sounded even lamer when I said it than it had in my head.

# CHAPTER FOURTEEN

*D*ay three of the great gold hunt got called on account of thundershowers, and on day four, everyone had something else to do. Able sold three picnic tables and had to deliver them. Without his brother-in-law twisting his arm, Bill couldn't be bothered to show, and Harley's youngest caught a stomach bug. In the interest of fair play, and because Martha assured him the town books didn't actually close until Monday when the fiscal year ended on a Saturday, Dad extended the search through the weekend.

My shoulders would have thanked him if they could speak. I did it for them, then spent the day hanging out with Molly and obsessively replaying in my head the events from the horrible date.

*—Boyfriend night?* A text came in from Neena Montayne, my across-the-street neighbor and close friend.

*Nope.* A fact I suspected she already knew since

she was the observant type and Drew's car hadn't been parked in my yard two mornings in a row.

Things had been awkward between us after my stunned reaction to his request to take our relationship up a notch. We hadn't had time to iron things out before he'd had to go out of town for a fitness competition. He still called every day, but he sounded distracted and distant.

—*Bertinos delivery in ten. You want company?*

—*Pepperoni with the spicy sauce?* I texted back.

—*Is there any other kind?*

—*Door's unlocked.*

She arrived in a cloud of mouth-watering scent, the soft drawl of the south in her voice, her dark hair curling from the heat and humidity. I could sympathize since mine tended to do the same if I didn't keep it ruthlessly tamed.

"Everly, darlin, tell me something good. I've been wallowin', and now, I'm in dire need of cheerful news."

Neena was entitled to wallow as she'd just passed the first anniversary of her husband's death. Hudson Montayne represented a lot of firsts for me as well. He'd been my first serious boyfriend back in high school, the first dead body I'd ever discovered, and my first ghostly encounter. Thankfully, Neena didn't hold the first one of those things against me, and she didn't know about the last.

She set the pizza box on the coffee table and followed me into the kitchen for drinks. "Still, I can take some pride in the fact that I didn't plumb the depths Viola went to."

While I sympathized with Viola Montayne's loss, some of her methods for handling her son's death had been a tad dramatic. Last Christmas, she'd paid a small fortune to have his face done up in lights on her house roof. I was almost afraid to ask what she'd done now.

I didn't have to because Neena was all too happy to lay out the details. "First thing she did was take out a two-page spread in the Bangor Daily to announce he was gone but not forgotten. Must have cost a fortune."

"I'm sorry, that must have been a difficult thing for you to look at." Viola wouldn't have considered whether her actions might be hurtful to Neena. She'd exited the womb with the empathetic capacity of a mosquito.

"Took me by surprise, I must say. I guess you didn't see it for yourself, then."

My papers for the week were still in a pile on the table next to the door. I hadn't had a chance to read them with everything else going on. "Not yet."

She went ahead of me into the living room, where we discovered Pearl had taken up residence on the warm top of the pizza box. "When did you get a cat?"

"Scat, Pearl!" I gave her a shove and flipped open the lid. Pearl had crushed the cover, so strings of cheese arched between the pie and the cardboard. "Oh man, would you look at that," I said. "What a mess. She's a nice cat, but her former owner spoiled her, and she hasn't any manners."

"Pardon my fingers." Neena tugged bits of cheese off the cardboard, pushed them back into place. "There, no harm done except for cosmetic damage." Most of her attention, however, was on Pearl. "She's gorgeous. Where did she come from?"

"She belonged to Delly Harper."

"Such a sad thing. He was a nice man." Neena spoke as if she'd known him, and I nodded as I set plates down beside the mutilated pizza. "He did something nice for me once."

"He did that a lot. Want to tell me about it?"

Between bites, Neena did. "It was last year, not too long after Hudson passed, and I'd locked my keys in the car while I was in the grocery store. It was raining, I had a half a gallon of ice cream ready to puddle, and I'd just had another run-in with Viola about something stupid. Hudson's guitar pick that I put in with his ashes, I think."

From mid-June, when Hudson was murdered, until Christmas, when a miracle put an end to it, Viola directed all her pain and suffering into a waged war with her daughter-in-law over every little thing her precious son might have touched. Sometimes loss tears families apart, and sometimes it pulls them together. Hudson's eventually did both.

"Anyway," she continued. "There I was, standing next to the car, feelin' lower than a grasshopper's belly button, and all I could think to do was call Hudson, which, of course, was the one thing I couldn't do. So, I just stood there, cryin' in the rain until I felt a hand on my shoulder."

While Neena talked, Pearl sidled back into the room and inched her way toward the sofa.

"'Now there, young lady, it can't be as bad as all that,' he said it so kindly that I blubbered out who I was and what had happened. My voice went so high I think only dogs could hear me by the time I was finished, but Delly just kept patting my shoulder, and he let me get it all out."

As if she knew her former owner was being spoken of with appreciation, Pearl edged closer still and finally crept onto Neena's lap.

"Once I'd calmed down, Delly used a piece of wire, and somehow—I think by magic—popped my door locks. He got me settled in the car, told me to take care of myself, and to never forget that love doesn't die even if our loved ones do, and then he smiled and was gone. I don't even remember if I thanked him."

"If half of what people say about him is true, Delly wouldn't have cared if you did or not. He was a man with a lot of heart." And once again, I pledged to do him right by figuring out who killed him. He deserved at least that much.

Absently, Neena reached down to scratch behind Pearl's ears, which set the cat to purring, and without even thinking about it, I said, "You could pay him back by giving Pearl a good home. You like her, and she seems to like you. She hasn't let me cuddle her like that, and I've been trying for days. She's not happy here."

"Do you think I should?" Neena seemed surprised. "Hudson didn't like cats much."

I grinned, and for once, knew something useful. "Hudson only said he didn't like cats because Viola professed to be allergic, but he fed a stray cat that came in and out through his window and basically lived in his room for an entire summer, and she never sneezed once."

She wanted to take Pearl; the need was written all over her face, so I pushed a tiny bit harder. "Hudson loved that cat, and when it stopped coming around, he searched for it for weeks. He loved you, too, and he'd want you to have Pearl for company. Just look at her; she wants you, too."

On cue, Pearl sprawled over on her back and presented more of her neck for Neena to scratch. "You are a precious one."

Just like that, the deal was done. "I have her things: litter box, extra collars, food, toys. You won't have to worry about a thing, and Molly thanks you from the bottom of her heart. She and the cat haven't managed to get past the armed truce stage."

"Okay, I'm sold. Now, to change the subject, what's going on with you and that fine hunk of man you've been dating? And don't tell me it's nothing because your face says otherwise."

Deep breath, and then I jumped right in. "Drew thinks it's time we took the next step." There, I said it. Out loud and everything. "He wants to move in with me."

Mid bite, Neena paused and put the slice of pizza back on her plate so she could turn and give me her undivided attention. "Wow. Just wow. And how did that make you feel?"

I had to laugh. "Well, Dr. Montayne, it made me feel..." The laughter stopped. "Weird, and scared, and happy, but mostly scared enough to make an utter fool out of myself."

Neena waved away the notion, "I'm sure you didn't."

"Oh, but I did." I didn't even have to close my eyes to see it all play out again: my stunned silence, his fading smile, the hurt in his eyes.

"I clutched, okay? I mean like totally and completely. Mouth hanging open, blank look in the eyes, which he took to mean I wasn't interested, and then it got awkward. We've been in a weird place ever since, and now he's out of town, so I need to figure things out while he's gone."

Eyes dancing, Neena picked her pizza back up and took a bite. "You know, I came over here feeling down, and frankly, a bit sorry for myself, but your misery has perked me right up again."

"Why, thanks. I guess. Glad to be of service." But I got what she meant. "The real question is, what do I do now? Do you think it's too late to fix things?"

Neena's paper plate landed in the now-empty box as she shifted the cat into a more comfortable position, tucked her legs under, and gave me her undivided attention. "Do you want him to move in?"

As if that question hadn't been running through my mind for the past two days.

"I don't know." And that was the problem. "He's been sleeping here more than his place for the past couple of months. Why the sudden need to make things official?"

The arched brow and pointed look stung a little. "Oh, I don't know. Maybe because he loves you, and taking the next step is what most women want. Or maybe he's being pragmatic and doesn't want to keep paying rent on a place when he's hardly ever there."

I covered my face with my palms. "Or both of those things. Why am I such an idiot?" The question was meant to be rhetorical, and when Neena opened her mouth, I cut her off. "Don't answer that."

She wagged a finger at me. "I wasn't going to agree with you. I only wanted to point out that you've been put through the wringer and then hung on the back of a chair to dry by that jerk you married."

She made a good point.

"But that's no excuse for closing your heart to someone who isn't Paul." For emphasis, Neena repeated, "Drew isn't Paul."

"I know that." My throat threatened to close up on me. "I do. I feel safe with Drew. Comfortable. Like we've already been together for a lifetime."

"Good grief, Ev, did you tell him any of that?"

"I don't think so. Why?"

"Men are like cats."

My tone went dry. "I thought they were from Venus. Or Mars, or something."

"They are like cats. No matter how soft they are and how loud they purr, and even if they sleep all day in front of the fire, a cat thinks it's a tiger. They expect you to respect their claws."

Her metaphor had a lot in common with scrambled eggs, but I guessed I understood what she was trying to say.

"I haven't tried to clip his claws. Maybe that's the problem."

Finally, leaving the cat analogy aside, Neena drilled right into the heart of things. "Do you love him?"

"I do, but we fell into a relationship so quickly that I can't help making certain comparisons to how things happened with Paul. With him popping back up at the worst possible moment, it's put me into a weird funk."

At Neena's insistence, I told her how Paul had courted me, how he'd swept me off my feet, and how my mother had pegged him as a mistake right from the beginning.

"If you tell her I said this, our friendship will take a rocky turn, but I wish I'd have listened to her at the time. Still, I can't go back and undo the past, and I wouldn't want to since it has led me back home, to this house, to new friends like you, and to Drew."

"But..." Neena knew there was one even if I hadn't completely sorted it out for myself yet.

"But...look around. I've been here a year, and I haven't made too huge a dent in clearing Catherine's things or in making this house my own. Now I'm just supposed to somehow make room for someone else?"

Plus, I couldn't tell Neena there were ghosts in and out of my place on a rotating basis, and that was a whole other complication. So far, Delly had been the most respectful of my personal space. He waited until I was in public to talk my ear off. Again, another complication, but one not related to Drew's proposed change to our living arrangements.

So now, I had to weigh the possibility of seeing more ghosts in the future against telling Drew about them before he moved in. How would that conversation go? I couldn't even imagine. Probably settle the whole moving in question quite handily, though, by scaring Drew out of wanting to take any more steps with me, and who could blame him?

"You know it's okay if you're not ready, right?" Neena interrupted my thoughts. "I'm not tryin' to push you into anything, either. I just thought maybe it would help you gain some clarity if you talked everything out." She reached over to pat me on the leg. "Now, about the house. Why are you holding on to Catherine's things?"

Before I answered, I took a moment to look at the room around me. I'd replaced the books on the shelves with my own, removed most of the knickknacks, and added more color with new curtains and pillows.

"I don't spend a lot of time upstairs because this is more house than I really need, and I've made inroads on this level. Catherine had good taste in furniture, so living with some of her choices isn't a hardship."

I looked around again with a more critical eye. "But this wallpaper is just," I hated to speak ill of the dead even to the point of criticizing her decorating choices, "it's hideous. I'd love to take it down and paint the walls a pretty color."

We spent the evening talking over ideas and making plans for redecorating the rest of the down-stairs. When she left, I had a handful of drawings she'd made and thought we both felt a little better for focusing our attention on something constructive.

"Nice, girl." Delly's head poked through the front door after I'd closed it behind Neena. Since he couldn't knock, I supposed he considered the minimal intrusion a polite compromise. "She'll take good care of Pearl. I think they need each other."

"She is, and I hope you will forgive me, but letting her take the cat seemed the right thing for both of them. What can I do for you, Delly?"

"You told me to come and tell you if I remembered anything, and I did, so here I am."

Sighing, I waved him inside, settled myself on the stairs so he'd take the hint that the hallway was as far as I wanted him to go.

"I'm glad you're here." Sort of anyway. "What can you tell me about Barrow's offer?"

"That?" Delly flicked his wrist to wave away the question as unimportant. "They're looking to sell the quarry, I guess. That section down behind the Jackson place belonged to Clint. He gave them a right of way to use it, and I expect they paid him for that, but Clint never said one way or t'other. They came around asking to buy out the right of way for enough to cover the taxes for the next five years, at least. I figured it was a good deal."

I noticed Delly never called Clint's house home. It made me sad.

"You should probably tell your father about the deal. They might still want to go through with it."

Gold digging madness would never have let Delly contemplate selling off land he thought worth exploring.

"You don't think the gold is there, then, I assume."

"Don't make no sense it would be if Clint sold off the right of way, does it?"

When he put it that way, I guessed not, and when he geared up to launch into one of his stories, I cut him off. "What did you come here to tell me?"

"Funny you should mention Barrow's offer because I did talk to someone about that, and it's probably not important, but it happened the same day I..uh...fell, so I figured you'd want to know."

"I do." I felt the little tingle that meant what he had to say was important.

He opened his mouth to speak, then closed it again, and frowned. "I talked to two people, come to think of it. Three if you count the nice girl in my lawyer's office. She just got back from a trip to the Grand Canyon. I always wanted to go there."

"Who did you talk to, Delly."

"Just Bill Cavanaugh at the bank. I had to get some numbers for something called a wire transfer. He asked why I needed them, so I told him how much Barrow wanted to pay, and he said I should ask for more. It was good advice because I did, and they went up another thousand. Like taking candy from a baby."

That's one of those phrases I find just plain weird.

What kind of a jerk do you have to be to take candy from a baby? And wouldn't it just make them cry? I say no to crying babies.

"I'm glad you told me, but I can't see where Bill would have a motive to kill you."

"I keep telling you no one had a motive to kill me. I lived by the Golden Rule and fell by accident."

And yet, he was still here. "You were—are—a good man. I'm just trying to figure out what happened so you can go into the light. Don't you want that, too?"

Nodding, he faded away. I wasn't sure what that meant, but it was time to go into research mode.

"Wow, Mom. Well done." I said out loud when I navigated to the library's updated website. There, in the sidebar, right where she'd told me to look, I found the link to the archives and ran my previous search. "Let's see what there is to see. What do you think, Molly? Will I find myself a killer?"

As usual, Molly's response was to snuggle closer and nudge her head more tightly against my leg. She sprawled across the cushions, taking up most of the space while I rested my feet on the coffee table and cradled my laptop against bent knees.

The house seemed calmer with Pearl gone, and I

wondered how she and Neena were getting along. I like cats just fine, but that one hadn't cared much for me and less for my dog, so we just hadn't been a good fit.

The search finished, and I clicked on the article to find the text readable but first, clicked again on the image and zoomed in until it filled my screen. Grace Belanger looked like a nice enough woman in the photo. I mean, she wasn't scowling or twisting an imaginary mustache or anything. She smiled with her eyes as she accepted a plaque that I couldn't read because the arm of the man presenting it covered the printing on the front.

Still, the more I studied her, the more she reminded me of someone else, and when I scrolled the photo out wide, it quickly became apparent who. Carlene Nicholson stood far enough away from Grace that only a little more than half of her had ended up in the frame. Looking back and forth between them felt like one of those spot-the-differences games.

Same hairstyle—cut and color—swept up and back into a chignon to show off graceful necks and similar pairs of dangling earrings. Teardrop-shaped for one, square for the other. Grace stood out in a wine-red dress that managed to be both figure-flattering and professional. The straight neckline and subtle pleating down the bodice cut back on the va-va-voom factor. Carlene wore the same color, though in a simpler, less expensive-looking fabric. Plus, Carlene couldn't have filled out a dress like Grace had on without significant facial tissue investment.

While Grace was quoted as giving profuse thanks to her team, Carlene received no mention outside of the photo caption, which said something about her contribution. Probably explained the tightness around her mouth and the sidelong glance directed at her boss and supposed mentor.

Carlene struck me as the type to toot her own horn and to expect others to blow the same tune. Where that attitude played in with patterning herself after her boss was a good question, though. According to my mother, Grace left town right after the event. Maybe Carlene knew what was coming, and that was the reason for the sourpuss. The only way to find out was to ask her, I supposed.

Great. Just what I wanted to do.

Then I noticed another name in the caption that I recognized. Maryann Payne faded far enough back in the photo that I hadn't noticed her at all. Well-dressed, she still looked somewhat dowdy in comparison to Grace. Her face—what I could see of it—held the same cheerful expression she'd worn the day I met her. I bet she rarely sported any other. She seemed the type to smile in the face of adversity.

We'd bonded over cleaning supplies. Why should I feel bad considering her as a source for information and impressions on what Grace had done? Something about the broker's disappearance rang bells in my head that no one else seemed to hear, and something about the photo nagged at me like a fragment from a half-forgotten dream.

Neither of which, I sternly cautioned myself, had anything to do with Delly's death. If I wasn't careful, I'd let Carlene's snippy attitude and my dislike for the same drag me down a rabbit hole that probably led to a chipmunk's house—as Grammie Dupree would have said.

Don't ask me to explain that one; it wasn't one of her better sayings.

# CHAPTER FIFTEEN

The clock on my bedside table read 4:38 when I bolted awake and scared Molly into letting out a startled bark, which then startled a yelp out of me.

"Sorry, Molls, but I just remembered what was bugging me." My bare feet hit the floor; I grabbed a robe and made it halfway to the door before I remembered I'd left my laptop on the desk in my bedroom. While Molly watched me like I'd been put on the earth purely for her entertainment, I flipped open the computer and tapped the power button.

While the computer booted, I tried to remember what I'd done with the earring I'd found at Delly's place the first day of treasure hunting. My body might be on the move, but my brain wasn't quite in the same time zone.

Shorts pocket.

Unconsciously, my hand mimicked the motion of dropping the earring in there. Then, I'd tossed the shorts into the dirty clothes hamper on my way to the shower after a day of sun and sweat. The hamper that now stood empty forced a detour to the laundry room where I checked the plastic bowl I used for throwing loose change and other pocket detritus.

No earring.

I flipped open the washing machine lid. Empty. Then I remembered I'd put the clothes in the dryer before I went to bed and figured I'd fold them in the morning. The shorts were, you'll know this if you have ever rooted through your own dryer, on the bottom because that's where things always are when you want them. I crammed my hand in the pocket, and again, no earring.

Yanking your own hair isn't the least bit productive in these situations, but it can relieve stress. Or not. In this case, not.

It wasn't at the bottom of the washer, but I found fifteen cents when I ran my hand around the drum. It didn't fall out of any of the clothes I shook out and hastily folded.

I finally found it in the lint trap, the hook jammed through the mesh of the screen.

Triumphant, I carried it back to the bedroom just in time to see my laptop go into sleep mode.

I let out another annoyed yelp and tapped the space bar to wake the thing back up. Honestly, sometimes nothing seems easy.

The clock on my bedside table read 4:57 when I held the earring up to compare it to the one Grace Belanger wore in the photo taken on the last night she'd spent in Mooselick River.

A perfect match.

Now, I had questions. Plenty of them, and as they flashed through my mind, the possible answers sent a whisper of trepidation to quiver in my gut.

What were the odds the earring belonged to someone other than Grace?

That one I thought I could answer. In a town the size of Mooselick River, the chances of two women owning the same pair of expensive earrings in such a distinctive design were about the same as a rainbow-farting unicorn running through town. This was Grace's earring; I'd stake my life on it.

Had she gone out to the Jackson place the night she left town? Why? And where was the other earring? Better yet, where was Grace now? Had anyone seen her since the night she left? What did Delly know?

The vague sense of unease continued as I pulled

on the first clothes that came to hand, headed to the kitchen to get a pot of coffee going since it was too late to go back to bed.

"Delly! Are you around? I need to talk to you."

If I had to be saddled with ghosts, it seemed like there should be a more reliable way to contact them when I needed to, but I guess a spooky phone system hadn't come with the package.

"Come on, Delly. It's okay to come inside. You have my permission." Of all the ghosts I'd met, Delly was the first to follow my rules about bugging me at home. I almost wished he wasn't such a stickler.

While I opted for cold cereal, Molly gulped her breakfast down in about two bites and then danced toward the front door to let me know she wanted her morning walk.

"Not today, sweetie, but you can come treasure hunting with me, okay?"

She might not know what treasure hunting was, but Molly understood the coming with me part, so she wasted no time doing her business, then indulging in a case of the happy wiggles while I grabbed my hiking pack out of the closet and prepared to pack a few things I thought I'd need.

First, a pair of gardening gloves went into the

pack for protection in case I decided to do some digging. I also added a cloth hat with a wide brim to keep the sun off my head and an extra container of sunscreen in case I ran out. This time, I planned to be better prepared.

A cooling neckband—an ingenious thing that absorbed water and stayed cool all day—went into a plastic container to soak during the drive. A thermos bottle of ice water, Molly's collapsible water bowl, and a couple of energy bars rounded out my supplies.

"There, I think we're ready," I said and only winced a little when I slung the pack over my shoulder. Some of Momma Wade's best liniment, the heating pad, and two days of not swinging the metal detector worked wonders, but not miracles, so I still carried a bit of soreness in the shoulder area. "Come on, Molls. Let's go see what the day brings, shall we?"

We stepped out onto the front porch to find Delly standing there, his eyes wider than usual.

"I came as soon as you called," he said.

"Why didn't you come inside, then? I told you it was okay."

He shrugged and cut wide eyes away from mine, his ghostly face going a shade darker in embarrassment. "It's early in the morning, and you're a single woman living alone."

"I was dressed before I called to you if that's what you were worried about, and you're a ghost. I think I'm safe enough, even if you were a creeper in life, and I don't think you were."

"A creeper?"

"You know, a lecher. A womanizer."

Shock and dismay washed over Delly's face, his eyes and mouth going wide and round. "I never."

"I know, Delly. It's okay. That's why I said you could come inside."

It's also why I'd dismissed Jacy's speculation Delly had been killed because of an affair gone wrong. "I'm headed out to the Jackson place. You can ride with me, okay? I have some questions for you."

He came along, but his response had already ruled out the more salacious possibilities. In the car, I decided to take the direct approach.

"How well did you know Grace Belanger?" I watched him out of the corner of my eye while keeping most of my focus on the road.

"Grace Belanger." He repeated thoughtfully.

"Grace Belanger. Worked in real estate with your cousin, Carlene. Might have done something shady with the land deals for the new road system. On the young side, pretty, left town in a hurry. Grace Belanger."

Delly frowned.

"Lost her earring near your place on the night she took off. Grace Belanger." I'll admit that last one was pure assumption on my part, but if the earring was hers, and she had them on at the awards thing, and she left town that night, it wasn't a huge leap.

"I'd go so far as to say I might have heard the name, but I can't put a face to it."

The dead don't lie. I don't think they can, but I'd have believed Delly even if he was on this side of the veil.

"Can you think of any reason she'd stop by? Clint's property isn't anywhere near where the new road went in. Maybe she wanted to talk to you about the inn. It would have been a while back."

"How far back?"

I gave him the date from the article.

After a short pause, Delly said, "I can guaran-damn-tee I never saw the woman that night. Not no way, not no how."

"How can you be sure?"

"Because I was down to Bangor in the hospital,

wasn't I? Having my gall bladder out. I spent a day and a half in the emergency room waiting for a bed, and then two days waiting for the doctors to decide what to do with me. The surgery didn't take half as long as all that. They put me in with a nice old fellow by the name of Bob. Helluva nice guy. Two daughters and a son. Three grand-babies between them. The son lives in Hollywood and does animations—that's cartoons, I guess—for some TV show."

Delly was on a roll, and once he started with a case of verbal diarrhea, there'd be no stopping or getting sense from him until he was finished. It didn't matter that his conversations daisy-chained from one to the next or that they didn't seem connected together. Once Delly got going, the only way to shut him up was...well, there wasn't a way to shut him up. The only thing to do was ride it out.

It was just a little after six before Delly finally faded out. Operating on a hunch, I called Drew.

He sounded sleepy when he answered. I felt bad when I looked at the time.

"I'm sorry, I didn't realize it was this early, and I know you got in late last night. Go back to sleep."

"I'm awake now. What's up?" I heard the rustle of

bed linens, pictured him there, and almost lost my train of thought.

"Listen, I know things are weird between us, and it's all my fault, but do you think you could come with me to the quarry, and maybe don't ask too many questions?"

"Is something wrong?"

"I don't know, but maybe."

"I'll be dressed in five if you want to pick me up on the way."

"That works, I'll stop in at the diner to grab coffee on the way, and Drew, thank you." I hung up before he could respond.

It occurred to me after I did that, he probably thought I was talking about us.

# CHAPTER SIXTEEN

Already dressed and waiting, Drew climbed into the car as soon as I pulled up in front of his place. He leaned over to give me a quick peck on the lips, but we didn't look each other in the eye.

"How was your flight back?" I am Everly Dupree, queen of awkward chitchat with soon to be former lovers.

"It was fine. What's wrong?" Direct and to the point. I could take a lesson from Drew.

"I think someone murdered a woman up near Delly's place two years ago."

Stunned silence met the bald statement, so I continued. "And I want you to help me find her. Or, I guess, what's left of her." A shudder-worthy plan if I do say so myself. But what else could I do? My gut practically stood up and danced because all the pieces fit.

"Why?"

My hands shook on the wheel as I steered onto

Delly's road. "I don't have the motive yet, but Grace Belanger left town without warning and under what I think are suspicious circumstances. But, since everyone blamed her for the road debacle, they all thought she bolted to save face. No one ever reported her missing."

"Not even her family?"

"I don't know. I haven't had a chance to look into that part of it yet. If there's no body, there's no reason to investigate."

He could have asked more questions. He could have turned the conversation to the topic of us. He could have been more like Paul and played a passive-aggressive game of making me feel like an idiot.

Drew did none of those things. He settled back in the seat, waited for me to park the car, and then followed me across the yard and toward the edge of the cliff. Reading our mood, Molly paced beside us, subdued.

"My dad and the others will be here in an hour or so," I told him. "We have to find her before they get here."

I headed for the fence between Barrow's land and Delly's and trespassed without so much as a tweak to my conscience. Delly hadn't shown up, and I didn't want him nattering away in my ear while I followed my instincts along the narrow ledge above the quarry.

You're not supposed to look down from great heights, but when the thing you're looking for is down, you do what you have to do. When I wobbled once, Drew caught hold of my arm. "Breathe from your center. Let everything else go." Steadied, I pressed on.

"There. Do you see what I see?"

"I see something fluttering. It looks like plastic sheeting." Drew leaned out, and I didn't breathe until he stood straight again. "There's a way down, but we have to go back to go forward."

He turned and gestured for me to go ahead of him the way we had come. On the other side of the fence, he took the trail down to the shallow section of the crevasse, ending up near where we'd found Delly's body.

Grimly, I followed his lead, felt the stretch in my calves as he skirted behind, around, and over slabs of slate, gradually easing upward until we came out on a narrow ridge about midway down the steep side of the quarry.

Around the final boulder, we found what I'd hope not to find.

Dirt clung to the tattered remains of the dress, and the tattered remains of the dress clung to what was left of the woman who surely must have been Grace Belanger. The sight of her took my breath away and would, I was sure, come back to haunt my dreams for years to come.

"That explains the earring." I looked away, tried to regulate my breathing so I wouldn't pass out or throw up. Either was possible at that point.

Whatever awkwardness we'd had between us faded when Drew pulled me away, turned me into his arms for comfort and protection.

"The what?"

"I think this is Grace Belanger." His chest muffled the words I had to force through a tight throat. It would have been easy to just stay in the circle of his embrace, sink into the feeling of safety and warmth, but Grace needed me more than I needed even a momentary freak-out.

Gently, I pulled back and away. Drew let me go, but slid a hand down my arm, clasped my fingers in his. "Was she a friend?"

"Never had the pleasure, but I know of her, and she's the reason someone killed Delly."

Drew's eyebrows went up at about the same speed my stomach headed south. Several four-letter words ran through my head, but I bit each one off before it shot out of my mouth, which would have been difficult anyway since my foot was taking up most of the space.

"Delly fell, didn't he? I thought Ernie deemed his death a tragic accident."

I sighed and tried to figure out how to explain without lying or actually explaining how I knew Delly's death was murder.

"I...uh..." My mind went blank. It churned out nothing but white noise and lost all connection to my mouth. "Well."

Just tell him, the angel on my shoulder said in my grandmother's voice. He's a good man. He can handle the truth.

I knew this moment would come eventually, but I didn't expect to be having it while standing next to the moldering remains of a corpse. Then again, the setting was entirely appropriate for coming out of the closet —or would that be coffin—as a conduit to the dead.

The timing couldn't be worse, given the colossal question already lurking between us. Then again, the devil on my shoulder reminded me, telling Drew my deepest secret would probably put an end to that dilemma. The devil also spoke in my grandmother's voice.

"Look, there's something I need to tell you, but before I do, can you just point out which direction I should take to get out of here?" My sense of humor gets a little weird in times of stress.

"If you think I would leave you alone in the woods with Grace or whoever she is, you don't know me at all. Maybe that's the problem. I'm not him. You can trust me."

Ouch.

My voice went soft with pain. "I deserved that." I pulled him away from the plastic-wrapped horror and toward a downed tree just the right height for him to sit, but I didn't let go of his hand. These might be our last moments as a couple, and if they were, I wanted to hold on for as long as he'd let me.

"This has nothing to do with Paul." Drew's eyes fired, but I held up a hand to stop him from speaking. "No, let me just get it out, and then, if you still want to be with me, we'll talk about our living arrangements."

Now that the moment was upon me, I couldn't think how to say what I needed to say. Should I take the rip-off-the-bandage approach or try to feed it to him in digestible bites?

"This is going to sound...strange, I guess, but you know Jacy's mom, right?"

"You know I do."

"Well, then you know she's a believer in all things...uh, spiritual, I guess is the right word."

Drew nodded, frowning.

"Okay, last year when Hudson Montayne was killed, you know I found his body, right? And then, well, I was upset, so Jacy took me to camp, and Leandra decided my aura needed clearing or something, and she did her woo woo thing."

"What does this have to do with us?"

"Everything. I'm getting to it, it's just hard to tell, and I know how this all sounds but anyway—" without thinking about it, my other hand came up, and I pressed fingers against the spot just above and between my eyes. "She put some stuff on my third eye. Oils and ashes, and I don't know what else, it's all a bit of a blur."

Anyone who knew Leandra would understand about the blur thing. The woman had that effect on people, and since the merest hint of a wry smile played over Drew's mouth, I suspected he'd had the Momma Wade treatment at some point in time.

The rest of the story was where things went a little nuts, so I took a deep breath and blurted it out in a long rush.

"She was only trying to help, but Hudson's...um... spirit...was still hanging around, and whatever she did made it so I could see him, and he wouldn't leave until I figured out who killed him. And since then, I guess you could say I see dead people, only not so much dead as murdered people. Well, except for that girl who was killed on her bicycle, because that turned out to be vehicular manslaughter, but that's how I know Delly was murdered." There was a short pause where I didn't dare look at Drew, and then I added. "Even if he doesn't think so."

By the time I got it all out, I was breathing hard, though that probably had more to do with fear than anything else.

When Drew let go of my hand, it felt like I might wither to dust and just blow away. I couldn't have uttered another word if my life depended on it because I knew the only word left between us was goodbye.

I turned away from him, slung an arm across my stomach to hold in the pain.

"Everly." His voice sounded so sad, so gentle. This was the kind of man who would always let a girl down easy, but I couldn't look at him while he broke my heart.

I hadn't wanted to feel like this ever again, but here I was, one year later, being dumped again. June just wasn't my month.

Drew spoke louder now, and his hand settled warm on my shoulder. "Everly, turn around."

"I can't. Just go, it's okay. I know the way back." I didn't, but I didn't care.

His hand tightened slightly, then moved down my arm until his fingers curled around mine.

Hope flared to life, but I ruthlessly tamped it back down.

"I'm not leaving you here."

"I said I'm fine." And I might have sounded more certain if I hadn't been sniffing back tears. "I don't need your pity."

Of all the things I expected to happen, being whirled around and yanked tightly against his hard body wasn't one of them. "Is Delly the only other man you're seeing that you haven't told me about?"

I looked up into blue eyes that twinkled with humor. Otherwise, we might have had a whole different fight on our hands. The bands that had settled around my heart to squeeze and pinch now broke and set me free.

"Well, there's the pizza guy, but our relationship exists on a purely culinary level."

He kissed me for a long time.

"I missed you," I whispered against his mouth.

"Me, too." He rested his forehead against mine, then let me go. "Is that it? Are there any more secrets buried in your deep, dark past that I should know about?"

My past wasn't all that deep or dark. It was the present that kept bogging me down.

## CHAPTER SEVENTEEN

Ernie didn't bother to use his words when we stood over the second body in less than a week. He leveled a look at me that said all he needed to say. I followed suit by pressing my lips together and giving him a shrug. What was I supposed to say, anyway? He'd believe whatever he wanted to believe.

Intermittent static coming from his communicator, the creak of Ernie's leather belt as he squatted were the only sounds I heard until plastic crinkled as he peeled it back from the body.

Finally, I couldn't take it anymore. "It's Grace Belanger, isn't it?"

Without being too graphic, I'll just say there wasn't much to go on besides the dress she had on and the second earring caught in a fold of the plastic. I recognized both.

"Based on the level of decomp, it could be. She's been dead at least two years."

"Murdered," Drew stated rather than asked.

Ernie nodded. "Pretty much had to be. The dead don't normally wrap themselves in plastic and throw themselves off cliffs." He'd already called in the medical examiner and the dead wagon. "Killer must have stashed the body somewhere else and then dumped her here recently. She hasn't been out here for too long. I'd say a week or less."

"How can you tell?" Since he wasn't reading me the riot act for once, I was happy to let Ernie talk. Somehow, this body tied to Delly's death, and the more I knew, the better I could help get justice for him.

"Couple of things. You've got your plants and foliage and such underneath the plastic—see how they're pale but still green? They'd be dead if she'd been here the whole time. Then there's the plastic itself. This here's your common low-density poly-ethylene. It's dirty and wet from the rain we had, but it's still intact. Two years of exposure to the elements dries this stuff out and turns it into confetti."

"What if Delly caught someone out here trying to dispose of Grace's remains? Don't you think tossing him off the cliff would be a good way to cover their tracks?"

When Ernie allowed the possibility, I gave myself points for biting back an *I told you so,* except my expression might have given me away because his tone turned acid.

"Or it could have been Delly doing the tossing, and he fell on his way back to the house."

"You're not serious? You can't possibly think Delly would commit murder. You were at his funeral. You heard all the nice things people said he'd done for them. The man was practically a saint. He was harmless, and he was your friend."

Ernie shrugged. "Guilty consciences spark just as many good deeds as shining hearts. People aren't always what you think they are, and yada yada yada."

"I think your job has made you jaded. Besides, Delly has an alibi for Grace's murder. He was in the hospital having emergency surgery when she went missing." When Ernie shot me an incredulous look, I hastily covered. "My dad has been sorting through his things."

Not a lie. Not a truth, either. I let the deception stand even if I felt slimy for doing so.

"I'll check into it," was all he said.

After using his phone to take a bunch of photos of

the body from every direction, he turned to Drew and asked, "You got a weak stomach?"

"I'm good."

"Okay, put these on." He slapped a pair of latex gloves into Drew's hand. "Now, give me a hand getting rid of some of this plastic so I can see what we're dealing with here."

While they were at it, I took hold of Molly's leash and wandered some little way from the activity because I really didn't care to see the rest of Grace. I also didn't care to meet her in spirit form—should she decide to present herself to me—with Ernie ten feet away.

Minutes passed while I waited, barely listening to Ernie's comments about the state of the corpse and the possible cause of death. Grace chose not to grace me with her presence—bad pun fully intended. Some small part of me felt slighted while the rest dared to hope she never showed up. One ghost at a time is enough. Trust me on this. I've been there.

"Everly!" Drew's voice finally broke through the near stupor I'd fallen into. "Ernie says we can go and that we can come down to the station tomorrow to make a statement. Your father is probably already topside and wondering where you are. We should go before he gets too worried."

"Oh, okay." I let him take my hand and lead me on the winding path back to Delly's house, where we broke the news of our grisly find.

"What made you decide to go snooping around the quarry?" His face gone ruddy, Bill Cavanaugh's nostrils flared like he'd stepped on a carpet made of rotten eggs.

I pointed a thumb toward where Drew rewarded Molly's good behavior by throwing a stick for her. "Just taking the dog for a walk." It really was my day for making deliberately deceptive statements.

"Well, I think we should call this whole thing off. It's clearly too dangerous to be out here. Two people have fallen to their death already. Isn't that enough?" He looked around, and his gaze fell on my father. "It's dangerous out here. You wouldn't want your daughter to end up like Grace, would you?"

Not giving my father a chance to answer, I said, "We've learned that Delly was about to sell off the section of land that borders the quarry. I think it's a fair assumption he would not have come to that decision if he thought there was even a remote chance of finding Clint's gold there. I think we can all agree that if Delly didn't consider that area viable, we can also rule it out."

Able nodded. Harley did as well. "Then we're agreed? We'll stay away from the cliff and concentrate our efforts a little closer to the house for the next two days."

"What about him?" Brow beetled into a frown, Able cocked his head toward Drew. "The rule is one helper per person. If he stays, that's cheating." He directed his criticism toward my father. "You don't want to be the kind of person whose word isn't worth spit, do you?"

"He's not staying," I broke in to forestall a verbal sparring match. "As soon as he's done playing with the dog, I'll send them both home."

"Are you sure you don't want to go with him, honey?" Dad pulled me into his side, spoke low, so only I could hear him. "Escape while you can."

"It's okay. I could use a day of mindless physical labor." The stakes in finding a killer were higher than ever.

"If you're sure."

Drew left, but finding Grace cast a pall over the search. Two hours in, all we had to show for our efforts was thirty cents in loose change and a cache of rusty tractor parts that had set more than one heart thumping when the detector emitted its low beep in seven different spots within just a few feet of each other.

Watching the anticipatory smiles slowly slide off the men's faces as first one, then the next sites yielded twisted hunks of metal that no one in their right mind would mistake for a buried fortune tugged at my heart.

"I thought we had it." Able mopped his sweaty brow. "I really thought we'd finally done old Delly proud."

"I thought I'd be getting that new transmission in my truck." Harley shrugged off Able's dagger-thrown look. "Oh, climb down off your high horse. Delly wouldn't care what I did with the money, and I don't see you planning to build a shrine to his good name."

Able bristled, and my dad stepped in to mediate. "This isn't how Delly would have wanted things to go. He chose the three of us because he knew we would work together, and he didn't put stipulations on any benefits we might gain. What would you do with the money, Able?"

We were spared the answer when a car pulled

into Delly's drive and disgorged Carlene Nicholson of all people.

"What's she doing here?" Able said what we all were thinking as we headed back toward the house to meet her.

"You'll all need to leave now. I've decided to exercise my rights as next of kin and take control of the property."

I glanced at my dad to see how he would take this turn of events. It's easy to gauge his mood because when his blood pressure goes up, his scalp tightens and makes his hair poof up. Carlene's news didn't seem to be having that effect.

If I'd been taking bets, my money would be on the fact that Carlene had remembered the Barrow offer and decided there was a little money to be made after all.

"It's nice to see you, Carlene. I'm sure Delly would be happy to know you've had a change of heart."

Thinking she'd won, Carlene's head popped up so high I could see up her nostrils. Pretty sure I could see right into her empty head, too.

Then my dad lowered the boom. "However, if you'll recall, you signed away your rights and responsibilities for his estate. Now, you're welcome to stay and join our efforts. I'll even give you my portion of the proceeds minus any residual costs for Delly's final expenses, but we're not going anywhere."

Grammie Dupree used to talk about people being madder than a wet hen. I've never seen a wet hen, but I can imagine what one would look like after watching Carlene's reaction. She let out an annoyed squawk, strutted around on heels too high for rural living, and issued a series of empty threats that my dad returned with his most implacable smile.

Even then, his hair stayed smooth, so I assumed he'd already spoken to Delly's attorney about the possibility that Carlene might try something. Whatever he'd learned, her tantrum failed to produce the desired result even when she devolved into name-calling.

"I told you to go. You're trespassing. I have every right to call the police and have you forcefully removed."

"That you do not." My dad's voice whipped out harder than I'd ever heard it. I glanced behind me to see both Harley and Able's stone-faced looks, Junior and his brother trying to hold back grins, and Bill looking bored. No one took a step toward her, or away from her, for that matter, but Carlene backed down.

"We'll see about that," she warned, then got back in her car and left.

"That was fun, huh?" Harley's tone was grim. "Do you think she'll be back?"

"Unlikely," my dad replied. "Delly's attorney showed me a property appraisal that was done about a year ago. There's no value here to speak of. Hasn't been since Barrow's closed down."

With Barrow looking to sell off the quarry, maybe things had changed. What if, I thought, Carlene had learned there was some monetary value to the property after all? That might be enough to cause this change in her tune.

I needed to tell my father what I knew, but not in front of everyone. It could wait until the drive home or maybe until I'd had time to do a little sleuthing first.

Before noon, dark clouds scudded in to blot out the sun.

"Rainiest June in a century." Able sounded like Eeyore as he made the dire pronouncement. Calling it an early day would free up some time I could spend investigating, so I welcomed the dampening mist that soon began to fall.

# CHAPTER EIGHTEEN

*W*orst one, first one.

Anytime a job needed doing, Grammie Dupree said it was best to start with the worst task first, get it out of the way early, and it was all downhill from there. Grammie Dupree hadn't had to choose between talking to Carlene Nicholson or Maryann Payne.

One was a horrible excuse for a person. The other was chatty enough to burn half a day and still not get any information. Not that those two things really compared. Maryann would win every single time.

Plus, with Maryann, I had a solid way in. Leo had decided he was interested in the house near the one on Tulip and asked me to drop by her office to pick up a spec sheet. Given the speed of the gossip network in Mooselick River—and the fact that Carol Ann Wilmette had been working dispatch when Drew called in to report Grace's death—the news that I'd found her probably got back to town before we did. If Maryann was plugged in at all, I wouldn't have to say a word to get her started on the topic.

Two minutes into the visit proved my theory right.

"Oh, you poor thing," Maryann jumped to her feet, came around the desk, and offered me a hug like she'd known me since forever. "I can't imagine what you must have thought finding Grace like that," she said once she let me go. "I don't know what I would have done in your place." Wide-eyed, she shook her head slowly. "It's just awful to think of her out there all alone all this time."

For all I knew, Maryann could have made it big on Broadway, but I just didn't get the acting vibe from her.

"Oh," I feigned ignorance. "Did you know Grace?"

"Oh, sure." I let her get me coffee, not because I wanted any, but because she didn't bother to ask. She just poured two cups, doctored them both the same, and led me over to one of the chairs in the waiting area. "I worked with Grace right before she...well, I guess, right before it happened."

I sipped the brew and found it bitter as Maryann

took her coffee with a splash of skim milk and nothing more. Maryann wanted to talk. I didn't have to pry too hard for the answers I needed because she held nothing back.

"Everyone said she left town because of some shady dealings to do with the land deals for the new road system, but I always thought she left because of man trouble. I heard her talking to Bill on the phone that day, and it sounded like they were in a fight."

"Bill?" The name gave me a tingle.

"Cavanaugh from over at the bank. They'd been seeing each other for quite some time, but I think they were on the outs." Maryann nodded sagely. "All the signs were there. Like he wasn't calling as often, and when he did, she wouldn't always talk to him. She didn't smile as much, but mostly, you could see it in her eyes. They looked haunted. Do you know what I mean?"

I did, but not for the reasons Maryann meant.

"But she never said a word to me. If she talked to anyone about it, she would have told her shadow."

"Her shadow?"

Maryann crossed one leg over the other, and her tone changed. "Yes. Carlene Nicholson stuck so close to Grace, not even her own shadow could get between them. If Grace farted, Carlene felt the breeze."

Hearing those words come out of the mouth of sweet Maryann nearly made me choke on my coffee.

"Tell me how you really feel," popped out of mine, and she gave a rueful grin.

"I'm sorry if that seemed catty, but I really don't like Carlene." She tilted her head sideways and assessed me for a moment. "If you want the truth, I didn't like Grace much, either. Not to speak ill of the dead, but I worked hard to become a broker, and when the owner here retired, I was supposed to run the office. Two days before that happened, Grace walked in and took over."

Just like that, Maryann earned a spot on my suspect list. Professional jealousy was as good a motive for murder as any. Mild-mannered as she might be, everyone has a breaking point, and Grace could easily have pushed Maryann past hers.

I pictured Maryann with that ever-cheerful smile on her face, staring down the barrel of a gun and pulling the trigger or doctoring a cup of coffee with poison. It gave me chills.

"She left the office in shambles that took weeks to

sort out." Pursed lips gave me a good idea of what Maryann thought about that. "I feel bad for it now, but at the time, I called her a spineless bimbo who kept her ego in her underwear."

"You said people thought she left town because of some shady stuff around the land deals for the new road. Is there any truth behind the rumor? I mean, we know she didn't actually leave, but that kind of thing could speak to someone's motive for killing her."

"Pshaw," Maryann flipped her wrist in dismissal of that theory. "Nothing shady about it. The state practically threw money in people's faces to get them to sell, but you didn't hear that from me on account of the non-disclosure agreements. Which," she said with a grin, "I never signed, so I am not technically bound to honor."

"Oh, that's okay, I don't need the details. I'm just repeating what I heard. Even if she made enemies, it seems like someone should have reported her missing. Do you know if Grace had family?"

Before answering, Maryann got up to top off the coffee I didn't really want. "No idea. She wouldn't have mentioned anything like that to me since I didn't keep my nose pressed to her backside like Mini

Grace. Carlene, I mean. She'd know; you should ask her."

Cue an internal cringe.

"I doubt Carlene would tell me anything. She doesn't like me very much." Less now than before, if that was even possible.

Maryann rolled expressive eyes. "Carlene likes Carlene. The rest of the world, not so much."

"Fair point. Her hatred of me goes way back. I can't imagine why since I barely knew she existed until I stopped into the agency where she works, and she raked me over the coals." When I was already at a low point, I didn't add since the sore place she'd poked still smarted a little.

"You just have to know how to play her. First rule of sales is learning how to read a potential customer. With Carlene, you just have to make her think she's the center of the universe. Want me to show you?"

I probably couldn't stop her if I wanted to, so I shrugged and nodded. "Sure, I guess."

After a frantic search for her phone turned up nothing, I finally had to dial Maryann's number. The ringing came from her desk drawer. "Shoot. I remember dropping it in there earlier. I'd forget my head if it wasn't attached sometimes."

Carlene picked up on the second ring, her *hello* sounding annoyed over the speaker.

"It's Maryann, I just heard the news about Grace, and all I could think was how devastated you must be, so I called to see if there's anything you need. I'm so sorry, you poor thing. What can I do to help you through this terrible time?"

If I'd have been on the other end of the line where I couldn't see the expression on her face, I would have taken Maryann's concern as genuine. In my head, I changed her name to Scary Mary.

"What will I ever do without her?" Carlene wailed with plenty of drama but little sincerity. That one probably shouldn't give up her day job for a life in the theater.

"Have you spoken to her family yet? I figure if anyone in town would still be in touch with them, it would be you. You were like sisters, after all." Maryann laid it on thick, and Carlene soaked up the attention like a sponge.

"Well, of course, we were. She was just every-thing to me. The world stopped making sense when she left town."

Melodramatic much?

Then why didn't anyone report her missing? I

mouthed at Maryann, who nodded and then had to wait for Carlene to stop gushing about Grace to ask. If any of my friends went missing, I'd have set up camp in Ernie's office until they were found.

No, that's not true, I'd have been out beating the bushes, and I wouldn't have stopped.

"She never mentioned anything about her family, so I don't know if she even had any. I just assumed she left town for the same reason everyone else did. A lot of people were upset about the new road bypassing Mooselick River. You know what people are like in this town. So positively provincial. They never forgive or forget, so brokering those deals effectively ended her career."

There was a pause before Carlene's tone turned bitter. "And mine."

With that, Carlene cemented her position on my suspect list. She hadn't reported Grace missing, and revenge always made for a good motive. Plus, her claims of a sisterly relationship rang false to me. Close friends tend to talk about family. Grace not mentioning hers called a lot of things into question.

Since Maryann had her talking, I figured she could save me the trouble entirely and popped open the notes app on my phone. I typed in: Ask her about inheriting her cousin Delly's property. I showed the note to Maryann, who nodded and posed the question as soon as Carlene gave her the opening.

"You've had so much tragedy lately. Didn't your cousin die recently, too? It must be hard what with having to handle his estate right now. I heard a rumor that the Barrow heirs are in talks to sell off the quarry. Doesn't that butt right up to the Jackson place?" I should have known Maryann would be clued in. She was a shark in sheep's clothing.

Carlene's tone iced over. "Delmar Harper was no relation to me in any way that mattered. I've washed my hands of his estate, and good riddance. The pittance the Barrow heirs offered might have sounded like a fortune to someone like Delly, but it was an insult. One I'm sure Leland Dupree will snap right up and then use the money to slap a memorial bench in the middle of town."

My face felt hot, and I had to clamp my teeth down hard on my tongue to keep from saying anything when a derisive laugh burst out of the speaker. "The more I think about it, that's just what they ought to do. Put a plaque on it that says Delly Harper's Lazy Ass Never Sat Here."

"Too bad whoever killed Grace hadn't done the

world a favor and taken that piece of trash out at the same time," Maryann gave me chills when she'd hung up the phone. "I didn't think it was possible to despise her more than I already did. I don't see how that helped much."

"More than you think." I had other questions. Lots of them, but since she was still on my suspect list, maybe Maryann wasn't the right person to ask. The last thing I wanted to do was tip my hand and end up being the next person to go missing under mysterious circumstances.

Instead, I rose, gathered up the spec sheets I'd come there to get, and left the office with my mind racing through various scenarios in which either Carlene or Maryann might have committed murder. They both had their reasons.

Then there was the boyfriend angle to consider. I'd had Bill Cavanaugh right under my nose the entire time we'd been hunting treasure together with no idea he might be connected. He certainly hadn't given anything away with his reaction to the news of Grace's death.

Unless he had the emotional range of a toothpick, that alone was enough to tweak my suspicions.

Back in the car, I sent Jacy a text to tell her where

I'd been and that I had news. Seemed like a good idea to buy myself some insurance just in case poking around in years-old murder put me in a killer's crosshairs. It wouldn't be the first time that happened. At least if I went missing, Jacy would know where to begin looking.

# CHAPTER NINETEEN

Steam rose where cool rain met heated pavement and also coated the inside of my windshield. I had to crank on both the AC and the defroster all the way back to Curated Collections. I spent the whole drive watching my rearview in case the possibly murderous Maryann had decided to follow me and run me off the road.

Call me paranoid if you will, I can take it.

Dodging raindrops, I made the dash from the car to the back door of the shop, only getting slightly damp in the process.

"It's about time you showed up." Jacy greeted me with a mock glare.

Neena seconded the glare as she finished ringing up a sale. She hurried the customer out the door before turning to me, or maybe I should say, turning *on* me. "At least your exploits are good for business since everyone, and their aunt has been in here pumpin' us for the gory details. If only you'd seen fit to drop by and give us some. Or you know, maybe pick up a phone. You're losing friend points at an alarming rate."

An oversight on my part. "I know. I'll make it up to you. We'll do girl's night at Cappy's, and dinner's on me. You can order anything you want."

"Oh, so you did strike gold." Jacy grinned to let me off the hook and picked up her phone, presumably to text her husband, Brian, to warn him he'd be on his own with the baby for a few hours.

"Not yet." I shuddered. "I'm not sure I want to go back there, either." But I knew that I would because I had a suspect to grill—unless Ernie made an arrest, but I didn't see that happening this soon.

Despite their request, I glossed over the worst of the gory details, and still, Jacy's face went white. Before I could tell the rest—what I'd learned from Maryann and Carlene—her gaze tracked toward the window.

"Shoot." She looked panicked. "Everly, get out now. Or at least hide in the back until she's gone."

I looked out the window and saw Momma Wade pulling her grandson out of the back of the car. Hooked into the grapevine as she was, she'd know all about my brush with death, and she'd ask questions.

The kinds of questions that I didn't want to answer in front of Neena, who didn't know about my ghosts.

"Good idea." I hot-footed it toward the storage area. As much as I loved Leandra, now was not a good time for me to see her. After she asked all the questions, she'd probably declare I smelled of spirit, or my third eye had the ghostly blinks, or whatever, and then she'd break out her bag of tricks. The last time she did that, I'd begun seeing ghosts, and I did not want a repeat in case there was a worse option.

"Why?" Neena began to ask.

"Sage. Smoke. Woo woo. Bad."

"Got it."

The door opened and, bless her heart, Jacy did her level best to speed her mother along. She failed utterly, of course, but I had to give her an A for effort. While I waited, I settled down on a pile of boxes to think through this latest turn of events.

Means. Motive. Opportunity

I watch enough crime shows to know those are the keys to solving a murder. Ernie said some of the damage to Grace's bones could have resulted from a gunshot wound or the recent trip down the cliff. Until the forensic reports came back, he couldn't do more than speculate on the cause of death. I'd bet all of my current suspects either owned or could get hold of a gun. They're not hard to come by in rural Maine.

Based on what I'd learned of Grace, any one of the usual motives for murder was in play. Love, money, and revenge all had a place in her story.

Opportunity—well, two years down the road, that one was going to be a non-starter for me. Presumably, all three of my current suspects had the opportunity, but then, so did practically anyone else in town.

Even if Maryann was right and the state had thrown money around to alter the route to Hackinaw, money wasn't the only thing that mattered to some people. For some, owning land that came down through the generations was a point of great pride, and no one, not even Grace Belanger or the state could put a price on pride.

"She's gone." Jacy poked her head around the corner, glanced over her shoulder, and came close enough to ask in a low tone. "Is she hanging around?"

"Who?"

"Grace."

Oh, her. "No, I haven't seen her, and I hope you

didn't just jinx me. One ghost at a time is more than enough."

"What's Delly saying about all of this?"

"I haven't seen him since we found her." Yet another mystery and one I barely had time to ponder before we rejoined Neena and I finished telling them my story.

"What I want to know is, who started the rumor she did some dirty deed and then skipped town?" Neena gestured with her cup of tea, nearly spilling half the contents in her lap. "You figure that out, and I'm betting you'll find her killer."

"You also have to wonder what happened to all her stuff." Jacy settled the baby on her knees and watched him chew his fist. "Someone must have gone to a lot of trouble making it seem like she left. Seems to me that's not something most people could pull off on the spur of the moment." She arched a brow at me. "I know you could, Miss Organized, but you're a freak of nature. Anyone else would need to plan ahead."

I'd been so focused on the actual murder I hadn't thought of all that had gone into hiding the crime for so long.

"I think whoever killed her," I said, "buried her

out near Delly's place, and then when they thought he might dig too close to the spot, they decided to move her. He caught them in the act, and they pushed him off a cliff to keep him quiet."

"So, I was right." Jacy nodded smugly. "More than once, too. Numbers three, four, and ten on my list."

"Your list?" Neena didn't get it, so Jacy explained that we'd come up with a list of possible reasons for Delly's murder.

"Wait, wasn't his death ruled an accident? How did you know it was murder before the cops did?"

"Intuition."

"Lurid speculation."

Jacy and I answered at once, but neither response took the suspicious look off Neena's face. "I feel like you're hiding something from me," she went from looking suspicious to hurt.

"We're not." I lied. "We were just fooling around. We had no idea Delly's death was anything other than a tragic accident."

Not too long after that, I made the excuse that Molly probably needed to be let out.

"I'll pick you up at seven," Jacy said as I opened the door to leave.

"Seven?"

"For Cappy's, remember? You owe us dinner, and I'm planning to splurge. Since I'm still this one's meal ticket, I'll be the designated driver."

There were worse things than arriving at a bar in a hot pink minivan, and one of them was arriving at a bar in a hot pink minivan with Jacy behind the wheel.

## CHAPTER TWENTY

"Do you realize how long it's been since we had girl's night?" Jacy dragged a perfectly fried shrimp through a pool of cocktail sauce, then double-dipped it in a plastic cup of tartar sauce before she popped the whole thing in her mouth. "I'm surprised we got our regular table."

"I'm surprised we didn't need a bigger one since you ordered one of just about everything on the menu," I teased.

"I did not. Only the app sampler and a seafood platter. This is the first time I've indulged since I popped Peanut out." Jacy still called the baby that sometimes. "I couldn't decide what I wanted." She eyed Neena's plate. "Those wings look good."

"As long as you're not eating chili, I'm happy to share." Neena grinned.

"Am I ever going to live that down?" Jacy wailed. "It was one fart. It shouldn't have to haunt me for the rest of my life."

"The good ones always do," Patrea said. "And speaking of good ones—minus the fart reference—I have news." She reached into her purse, and pulled out a small box, laid it in the center of the table. "Chris gave me something."

Jacy, Neena, and I participated in a synchronized inhale. "Is that a ring? Tell me it's a ring," I said.

Eyes shining, Patrea flipped open the box.

"It's a ring. It's a fabulous ring." Neena reached for it, then stopped and gave Patrea a questioning look. At Patrea's nod, she snatched up the box. "Vintage setting, emerald cut diamond. It's absolutely gorgeous. Why is it still in the box? You said yes, right? How did he propose? Was it romantic?"

Patrea put up a hand to stop the barrage of questions and, as Neena passed the box to Jacy, answered them in reverse order.

"It's Chris, and it's me, so romantic is a subjective term, but yes, I suppose it was. I mean, he didn't bake it into a cake or any of that nonsense, but he did say nice things." She actually blushed.

"I said yes."

I'm sure our squeals annoyed the people at the next table, but it's not every day your friend gets engaged. Jacy handed the ring box to me. I admired it and then gave it back to Patrea. Before the box went back in her purse, the ring was on her finger.

"I didn't want you to notice it too early, is all."

Before meeting at this very bar during her enforced Christmas vacation in Mooselick River, bad relationship experiences had both Chris and Patrea convinced they weren't cut out for true love.

"What are you going to do about your living situation?"

Taking over the Christmas tree farm that had been in his family for generations meant Chris had ties to this town that went beyond making a simple choice between staying or moving an hour away. But Patrea owned her own law firm and a nice town-house in the city. They'd been making it work, and an hour drive wasn't exactly considered long distance in this part of the state.

"That's my other piece of news. As of today, I've officially closed my office."

After a few seconds of stunned silence, I had to ask, "Does that mean I need to find a new attorney? Josiah Caldwell is cranky and hard of hearing, but he's the only guy in town."

Patrea laughed. "Not anymore, he isn't. Also, as of today, he's retired."

"You're taking his place?"

"I am."

"And moving here to live?"

"I am."

More squeals earned us two sets of raised eyebrows, one scowl, and an invitation to hush up from the neighboring tables, but we didn't care.

"I close on the townhouse at the end of the month," Patrea said when things were quiet again. "How fast do you think we can put a wedding together?"

"Dang, girl. When you decide to change things up, you don't fool around."

"When it feels right, you just have to act." Patrea practically glowed. "And this does."

Whatever I'd have said next fell right out of my head when I noticed a couple dancing alone in front of the jukebox. Generally, the dancing didn't start until the band kicked in around nine, but Carlene Nicholson and Bill Cavanaugh were wrapped around each other, swaying to the music as if they were the only people in the room.

I set my wineglass back down on the table and stared to make sure it wasn't a mistake. Jacy noticed the look on my face, whipped her head around, and did a double-take when she saw what I'd seen.

"Is that—?" She leaned close enough to talk in my ear so no one else would hear.

"It sure is."

"What does it mean?"

All I could do was shrug. I hadn't had enough wine to become impaired, but two glasses were enough to fuzzy up my logic processors. "It means something. I'm not sure what, but it's probably bad."

I'd have probably cornered Carlene to ask a few questions if the odd couple hadn't left before we finished eating.

Instead, we laughed, danced, and celebrated Patrea's good fortune. Some of us a little too much.

In the glow of Jacy's headlights, Neena wobbled her way up the steps, caught her balance, then waved a hand over one shoulder to let us know she was okay. She fumbled with her keys, and when she finally got the door open, turned, and blew a kiss toward the car. She'd had far less to drink that Patrea, who'd slumped down in the seat almost as soon as she'd buckled her seatbelt.

"I'd better ride out with you to drop Patrea off," I

said as a gentle snore issued from the back seat. "Just in case you need help getting her inside."

"Are you sure?" Jacy clicked on the dome light to assess my condition. "You look steady enough."

"I'm only a little buzzed. I'll be fine, and it will give us a chance to talk about the bombshell that dropped earlier."

"Speaking of which, have you seen..." Jacy trailed off, glanced into the back seat. "You know...her hanging around?"

She meant Grace. "No. And come to think of it, the other one hasn't been around much lately, either. Not since." I wiggled my fingers, and it was enough for Jacy to know I meant since I found the body. We'd known each other long enough to have entire conversations without using actual words.

We got Patrea inside and thoroughly embarrassed Chris with an exuberant show of happiness for his impending marriage.

"Stellar ring. You did yourself proud there. Perfect for her," Jacy clapped a hand on his arm, stretched up on tiptoe to plant a kiss on his reddening cheek, then whispered loudly. "Hurt her, and we'll hunt you down like a dog."

We left him with a befuddled look on his face and giggled about it all the way to the car.

"Okay," Jacy said once we were back on the road. "The way I see it, and correct me if I'm wrong, but Carlene dating Grace's ex must have bumped her to the top of your suspect list."

"Totally gives her flimsy motive a shot in the arm. Until now, I thought she lost more from Grace's death than she gained. She claims they were like sisters, but she didn't report Grace missing, so that's suspicious, but she lost her job, which lost her some points."

"What about him, though? Seems like it would be easier to dump her than kill her." To extend the conversation, Jacy drove slower than her normal, breakneck speed. "And since no one reported her missing, I think we can rule out the death for insurance motive all the way around. Not that we'd have any way of knowing who would have benefited, or if she even had any."

"True enough. But I'm still having trouble with the logistics. Like, let's say Carlene is the killer. Ernie wasn't sure about the cause of death, but he did say it could have been gun-related. So did Carlene leave with

Grace that night? Somehow get her to drive out near Delly's place, shoot her, then dig a hole, come up with a roll of plastic, bury her, then go back and clean out her place before morning? All by herself. I can't see it. She doesn't strike me as having the spine for all of that."

"Do we know if anyone went looking for Grace the very next day?"

"No, not exactly the next day, but soon after, I think. Now that you mention it, Delly said he was in the hospital for a few days at the time Grace went missing, so it wouldn't have all had to go down the same night."

As we made the final turn onto the road back to town, Jacy said, "That changes the timeline a little."

"I've been watching men dig small holes out at Delly's place for days. I just can't picture Carlene managing one of that size by herself."

"Unless they were in it together. I bet they told her they wanted to be together, but Grace just wouldn't let go, but their love was too strong, so they had to get rid of her."

I'd had enough drinks to lower my filters some, so I merely snorted. "The tragic romance theory?"

"I guess. Why? What's wrong with it?"

"Plenty. Maryann said Grace had been ducking Bill's calls for almost a week before she went missing. It just doesn't fit."

"Fine. Shoot down my balloon." But Jacy grinned. "I'll just send up another." She tapped her fingers on the steering wheel. "Here goes. Grace is ducking Bill's calls. They've been fighting, he's annoyed, so he asks for a ride home from the banquet. They fight, things get ugly, she's dead. He drives her out to Delly's place, buries her, and the rest is yada yada."

"Yada yada?"

"Sure. He's alone and lonely; Carlene is the next best thing to Grace by her own design, so he uses her to fill the gap."

"Almost makes me feel sorry for the vicious skank," I said. "Almost."

"But you think it could have gone down like that, right? I mean, who else could it be?"

"Well, there was Maryann, but she's a problem for all the same reasons as Carlene. She lacks the physicality."

"Unless the two women were in it together," Jacy said. "They both had reasons to want Grace gone."

"I guess you're right." We'd pulled into my drive

by then. "After all this time, there's almost nothing to go on. As much as I hate to consider the possibility, Delly might be stuck here for a while."

# CHAPTER TWENTY-ONE

The sound of a lawnmower—my lawnmower to be exact—firing up outside my bedroom window was an unwelcome sound at what felt like the crack of dawn. I slitted one eye to check the time, which Molly took as a sign that I was awake.

Careful not to break the rules, she'd taken up a spot sitting next to the head of the bed with only her head resting on my pillow, her nose about an inch from mine. I reared back in surprise, and also so my eyes would focus on her face.

The sudden movement proved I'd had a drink too many the night before. Not enough to need Jacy's hideous hangover cure, but enough to feel like my head was full of sludge.

"Ack," I said, which apparently, in dog speak, translated into *I'm up*. Molly's whole body quivered, and since I was up, she launched onto the bed. All seventy or so pounds of her.

"Ack," I said again, which is about all you can say when a dog her size lands on you. With the lawn-mower circling, there was no way she'd settle in for a cuddle and let me snooze for another ten minutes, so I gave in and crawled out of bed.

In the time it took me to get to the back door, Molly made the trip there and back at least three times, nearly tripping me with every return.

"Okay, girl. Settle down," I said uselessly. Only one man would be running the infernal mower at such an early hour, and that man was one of Molly's favorite people. "Let me get the leash, would you?"

David cut the engine and dismounted the mower as soon as he noticed us standing on the back porch. I let Molly go and couldn't hold back a smile as she danced across the grass in a blur of sleek, chocolate fur. Her training held, and where she once would have planted her paws on his shoulders, she instead dropped to her haunches and waited for him to run fingers over her ears.

"It's early."

"So, sue me."

We traded greetings.

"Coffee?"

"Eggs."

When I glared at him, he ignored me, picked up the tennis ball Molly dropped at his feet and winged it into the back corner of the yard. Knowing resistance was futile, I went back inside to fire up the coffee maker and pull a skillet out of the cabinet.

David wouldn't have come over to mow my lawn so early if he hadn't had a better reason than simply to get on my last nerve. We'd moved past the point in our friendship where he set out to annoy me on purpose, so I guessed I could make nice with some breakfast and listen to his troubles. He'd have done the same for me.

Fifteen minutes later, he opened the back door to let a panting Molly in just as I slid a perfect pair of over-easies onto his plate. "Your timing is perfect. You must have a sixth sense for when the eggs are done."

"And you're speaking in actual sentences, so you must have had enough coffee to be awake."

How well we'd come to know one another.

"Awake enough to know you're here for more than just the satisfaction of cutting the grass. What's up?"

"I found something at the inn that I think you should see."

"Okay. Well, I'm supposed to be out at Delly's by ten, and now that I'm up so early, I could use a shower. Can this wait until later?"

"Oh, I think you should come take a look now. Just trust me on this, okay?"

"If it's so urgent, why all the mowing and making me cook breakfast?"

He gave me a cheeky grin. "Twofer. It's fun getting you all riled up, and I was hungry. Besides, it might not have occurred to you, but you know I'm a guy, right?"

"I'd noticed." Even if he wasn't my type, David had all the right parts in all the right places to turn a girls' head.

"Then you should have let me take a turn hunting for treasure. That's a guy thing."

"Beg to differ, and still no reason to make me suffer. I could have slept for another hour."

He stood to rinse his plate and put it in the dishwasher. "Beg to differ," he mocked. "I'll come back and finish the lawn later."

"Tell you what. You show me what you found. If I think it's useful, I'll see if I can fix it so you get your shot at hunting for buried treasure. Deal?"

"Deal."

Harley and Able would squawk, but I figured I could work my way around them, and if not, my dad was the final authority. Even if we found Clint's gold, I didn't plan on taking a single nugget of it. So, as far as I was concerned, the only gold worth anything had been Delly's heart. The rest was just hunks of pretty metal. Not worthless, but worth far less.

At the inn, I followed David through the kitchen to a door I hadn't noticed before. It opened on a set of narrow stairs leading up into darkness.

"Hang on, I've got a flashlight," he said and went back to grab one big enough to be used as a weapon. Then he nearly blinded me when he flipped it on. "Sorry. At the top of the stairs, go left. I'll be right behind you."

The stairs let out at a short hallway with three doors.

"I think these were the family's living quarters. There are two bedrooms, a bathroom, and a small sitting room tucked in up here. They'd go down to use the kitchen, but these rooms would be where they went to have some private time."

I thought it odd Delly hadn't shown up to tell me all about this room in minute detail but didn't have time to dwell on why because David directed me toward a storage cabinet set in the wall beside the fireplace flue.

"Open the door and take a look."

I did as he asked and saw nothing but an empty cupboard with yellowed paper lining the shelves.

"Okay. It's nice. If that's all you dragged me over here to see, I'll be going now, and you can forget about hunting for gold."

David laughed. "See, I missed it the first time I looked in here, too. Look at the back of the cabinet door."

When I saw the house and surroundings sketched on the rough wood, I let out a low whistle. "Holy cats. That's the Jackson place."

I closed my eyes to picture the house as it was now, then opened them again to compare my mental image to the sketch before me. The two were different as night and day—I could almost imagine the downhill slide in time-lapse.

"Whoever drew this did a fantastic job. This," I pointed to the central part of the house, "Is all that's left of the place. That whole addition is gone now. There's nothing but scrub grass where this cute little garden area used to be. It's sad, really, to see it in its heyday and to know how far it's fallen since then."

When I turned, David wore a sad expression that seemed out of place for him since he didn't have the same frame of reference as I did.

"What's wrong," I asked.

"Nothing. I thought I'd found a clue that might help your dad in his search. I guess not, and now I've incurred your morning wrath for nothing."

"Hold on. Let me get a closer look. Someone drew this here for a reason. Can you take the light and shine it down, so it doesn't glare?" I passed it over, and then, when inspiration hit, took out my phone and snapped a photo. "Turn off the flashlight." He did, and I snapped another.

The low light settings on my phone's camera worked a minor miracle, making the drawing stand out from the grain of the wood and revealing more of the fine detail.

"See, there's a bench off to the side in this cute little garden area, and look how the artist used those fine half-circles to suggest the shape of those bushes with the big, ball-shaped flowers that can be pink or blue."

"You mean hydrangeas?" Leave it to David to know.

"Yes! Those ones." I spoke a little too loud. "Can

they grow into full-sized trees, though?" I got a little tingle in my fingers and toes. This was something. Something big. "There's a line of trees with flowers like that at the cemetery where my grandmother is buried. I don't think I ever put them together with the shrubs running along my mother's front porch."

David shrugged. "I think so."

My phone rang. I looked at the caller ID and cringed.

"I have to take this."

"Tell me you have good news," Martha's voice sounded strained when I answered my phone, which I knew was a mistake as soon as I did it. "I'm not sure how much longer I can keep this event running if we don't have something to report soon."

Maybe if Martha didn't seize even the most obscure opportunities to drum up tourism, she wouldn't be stressing out over every little thing. Saying that to her probably wouldn't curry me any favor. I wasn't sure I cared.

"I'm not sure what you want me to say, Martha. This event was your idea, not mine. I've got enough on my plate what with all the chasing of wild goose."

The sigh that gusted out of her didn't do a thing to decrease my annoyance. I'd already been disturbed far too early, had a minor hangover, and would be spending the rest of the day hunting for a murderer. What more did she want from me?

It didn't help that David found my half of the conversation amusing.

"At least stop by on your way through town. I could use some new ideas, and as our resident expert, I just know you'll come up with something exciting to take this event to a new level."

If I didn't, she'd just keep calling.

"Ten minutes. That's all I can spare." I hung up before she could argue for more.

"You've earned yourself a round of treasure hunting. You head out there, tell my dad I've got a quick errand to run, but I won't be too long."

A fine goal. Just not an attainable one.

# CHAPTER TWENTY-TWO

"Do you see what I'm up against?" Martha wailed. "Our turnout is lower every day, and we're barely in the black on this one. What should I do?"

*Let one opportunity go by. Have a drink. Maybe a tranquilizer. Untwist your knickers for a minute.* Inappropriate answers scrolled through my head, and I bit them back, one by one.

"I don't know. This may not have been the best piece of town history to spotlight. A man is dead, after all. Don't you think using his death to draw in tourist money is a tad unseemly?"

Maybe I didn't bite all of them back, but I did moderate my tone to be less insulting. Martha didn't see it that way.

"Are you calling me insensitive?"

Not in so many words.

"I wasn't trying to hurt your feelings."

"Then I guess we'll just chalk that up to one more

thing you're really good at," Martha sniffed, and I felt bad for sort of snapping at her.

"I'm sorry." I put my hand on her arm and gave her my most sincere expression. "There's no excuse for saying hurtful things, and I won't make one. Please accept my apology."

"I suppose you're forgiven. Now, what can we do to save this event?" Perky now that she had me on the ropes, Martha circled right back around to her original question.

So, I pulled something out of my...uh...hat. "Run a contest, and give away something fun for a prize."

Martha's eyes went wide and round to match the O shape she made with her mouth. "That's a fantastic idea. Why didn't I think of it?"

When she turned to bustle off and make the new plan happen, it occurred to me that I had before me the most eminent source of gossip in Mooselick River. And she owed me one, so I should make the most of the opportunity to weasel some information out of her.

"Martha, wait." I caught the annoyed look in her eyes as she turned. "What can you tell me about Grace Belanger?"

The first thing she told me didn't even require

words. The look on her face said it all. "She wasn't a very honest person. We figured that out right before she left."

"Before?" My mother had said after.

"Well, the same day, anyway. Paperwork came through the town office on the land deals, so I made a few calls and found out what she'd done."

"Before the banquet, not after?"

Martha tossed her head. "Didn't I just say so? We didn't want to make a scene, so we let her accept her award, but there would have been repercussions if she hadn't up and died. Not that we knew she had at the time."

"Who is we?" My sleuthing senses tingled like I'd touched a live wire.

"What do you mean?"

"You said *we* let her accept her award. Who else knew?"

"Oh." She put a hand to her mouth while she thought about it. "Well, there was me, of course, and the selectmen, because I called them to see if there was anything they could do to put a stop to the treachery. That's why none of the three of them attended the banquet. Too many phone calls to make, even to the Governor."

"Is that all? Just you and the selectmen?" She clearly hadn't activated the grapevine, or my mother wouldn't have mistaken the timing. It also seemed Martha could keep a secret if sufficiently motivated, which was news to me.

"I think so. I think someone was in the office when I got the call, but I can't honestly remember now. Once I knew what we were up against, I got all flustered, and I didn't want to start a panic until we'd taken every possible precaution. You know Grace was an outta-stater." Outta-stater is Maine speak for someone who lives in another state. It's often considered an epithet when it applies to someone who moves in and promptly gets involved in town business. Given Martha's tone when she used it, she meant it as an insult.

"I didn't know that. I knew she wasn't from around here, though. Was there anything else you could tell me about her?"

"Not that comes to mind. We tried everything we could think of before we went over to her place to talk. I was ready to throw the town on her mercy if that's what it took, but she'd packed up and gone. Turns out, she had one of those month-to-month leases, so we figured she hadn't planned to stick around long anyway. People weren't any too happy with Leo for not giving us the heads up."

More new information. "She rented from Leo?"

"Sure. That little one-roomer he has over behind the bait shop."

I knew the one she meant. "The furnished studio."

"Why do they call it a studio? Sounds pretentious, doesn't it?" Martha sneered, but I suspected her attitude had more to do with Grace than the term studio apartment.

"Anyway, I don't like to speak ill of the dead, but as far as I'm concerned, Grace Belanger was the devil."

With a request that she call me if she remembered who had been in the office the day Grace died, I let her get back to her event planning and contest. She'd just given me another avenue to pursue more information. My next step would be to visit Leo's office to look at Grace's lease.

I made it halfway back to my car before my plans got interrupted again. If I'd been paying more attention, I wouldn't have slammed into Ernie Polk when I hurriedly turned into the parking lot.

"Sorry, I wasn't watching where I was going. Are you okay?"

"Aren't you supposed to be slogging away in the gold mines?" He rubbed the spot where I'd poked him with my elbow.

"No doubt. Did you find out anything more about Grace?"

"Got preliminary cause of death, but I probably shouldn't tell you."

"You will, though, won't you?" Flirting used to work on him, but lately, he'd become immune to my charms. Going through certain experiences was probably the reason.

"Choked. From the front. Manually. Are you happy?"

"Do you take me for some sort of ghoul? Of course, I'm not happy. A woman is dead." I still shuddered every time I remembered how I'd found Grace. "Manually, that means someone used their hands. It was ruled a homicide, right?"

"Inevitably." He cocked his head to the side. "We didn't use to have homicides around here until you came back to town."

"You're singing the same old song," I said,

annoyed. "I don't kill people, and you know it. Can we just please admit the timing is a coincidence and move on?"

The squawk of his two-way saved him from having to commit to an answer, but the timing couldn't have been more perfect. I listened to Carol Ann tell Ernie someone had found a late model Prius in an abandoned barn halfway between here and Hackinaw. The car had been registered to one Grace Belanger.

That's how Carol Ann said it. One Grace Belanger. As if we were overrun with women by that name or something.

"I suppose you'll blame this on me, too."

"What if I do? You don't think it's a bit suspicious that you find her body, and then conveniently, Grace's car shows up? I ought to haul you in for questioning."

"But you won't because you're a good cop and a good man, and even if you won't admit it, you're glad I found Grace because you want to give her justice. That's why you do what you do and why you're good at your job. Any suspects? A work rival or jealous lover, maybe someone from her past?"

"Nothing's popped so far."

"It's been two years, and no one reported her missing," I said. "Doesn't that seem weird to you?"

Ernie shrugged. "I could quote statistics about how many bodies turn up every year that don't match any missing person reports, and no one ever claims. It happens more often than you think. Now, I have to get her car turned over for processing."

He wouldn't take me on a ride-along to look at Grace's car even if I asked nicely, so I didn't bother.

Besides, I had other clues to chase, so when Ernie's cruiser went left out of the parking lot, I turned right and headed to Leo's office to take a look at Grace's lease. What I saw there had me reaching for my phone.

Maryann picked up on the second ring.

"It's Everly Dupree. Are you busy?" Stupid question since I could hear noise, and she sounded distracted.

"I'm in town watching kids dig for treasure."

"Really?" Color me surprised. "Stay there. I'm five minutes out, and we need to talk."

"Okay." I bet she popped out of bed with that cheerful smile on her face.

It took a minute longer than the predicted five, but I found her near the sand tubs watching the kids, chatting up the parents, and handing out business cards. Ah, okay. Now, it made sense.

"Do you have a minute?" I couldn't tell if she'd volunteered to help or was just hanging around to drum up business. "This won't take long."

"Sure, one sec." She tagged someone else to take over, thus proving it had been the former. "What can I do for you?"

For privacy, I pulled her off to the side. "You said you heard Grace fighting with someone on the phone. Are you sure it was Bill?"

Lips pursed, Maryann took a moment to think and remember. "I thought it was because it sounded like a relationship fight, and they were dating, but now that you ask, I guess it could have been someone else."

I lowered my voice and leaned closer. "Like a husband, maybe?"

"No, she wasn't—" Maryann broke off when I gave her a raised eyebrow and nodded.

"Yes, she was. I got a look at her lease."

After hearing the cause of death, I no longer considered Maryann a suspect. Choking someone to death is not a job for a woman her size. It felt good to rule her out.

"Well, doesn't that just make your tea go cold?"

"Indeed," I said. "You had no idea?"

I got a slow head shake. "She didn't act married."

"Some people don't." I surprised myself with my lack of bitterness, given how well that truth had been driven home for me. "Did you hear anything to indicate she might be in danger from whoever was on the phone?"

"She sounded mad, not scared. You ask me, the person on the other end of the line had a better chance of ending up dead than Grace." Maryann tilted her head and asked the question that had been running through my mind ever since I got a good look at Grace's lease. "If she was married, why didn't he report her missing? Do you think he killed her?"

The husband's name was listed as a contact on her lease, complete with a phone number and address. If I found him that easily, Ernie probably had, too. He would not only beat me to making the call but be annoyed with me if he caught me prying. I'd have to wait until he checked the man out and bug him to tell me what he learned later.

"Could be," I said.

After chatting a few more minutes and learning nothing new, I made my excuses and left Maryann to go back to fishing in the kiddie pond for parents looking to buy or sell a home. Plus, I'd caught sight of Martha heading in our direction and decided I'd better make myself scarce before she dragged me into another lengthy conversation.

To that end, I ducked behind a cluster of people and mentally mapped out a circuitous route to my car. One that took me past what Patricia liked to call the plastic outhouses. One that I would come to regret within the next two minutes.

"I can't believe he had the nerve to question you like that." I didn't know the woman speaking by her voice.

But the strident, almost nasal tone of the woman who answered, that one I knew. "To think I'd do anything to hurt the best friend I ever had—it's ridiculous to the extreme."

"Hey!" said no-name. "I thought I was your best friend."

I could almost hear Carlene's eyes roll like beady green marbles. "You got any cigarettes? I'm dying for a smoke."

"You know there's no smoking at these things."

"We'll go behind the porta-johns where Martha Tightass Tipton won't see a thing."

Except I was back there and didn't want to be seen, either, so as the two women went around one side, I slipped around the other. Only on this side of things, the ambient noise level was higher, and I couldn't eavesdrop on them so easily. So, I did what any intrepid sleuth would do and stepped inside the toilet closest to the middle.

I realized my mistake when the smell hit me, but then I heard Grace's name and decided I had to stay. There aren't many mysteries in life that I feel compelled to solve unless a ghost's future is riding on them, but I needed to know what the last person to use this plastic outhouse had eaten so I could avoid it like the plague. It smelled like they'd tucked into a meal of rotten wildebeest carcass with a side of fermented beans. The big kind, with lots of whatever it is in beans that makes for hideous smells.

Shallow breaths kept me from gagging, but only just, and when I pulled my wandering attention back from my nose to my ears, I heard Carlene's friend pose a chilling question.

"Did Bill know she was married the whole time they were going out? Maybe he found out, and that's why he killed her, which means you're dating a murderer. OMG, you have to tell someone. Turn him in before you're the next one to die."

"Good grief, woman. Drama it down a notch. Grace wasn't married the whole time, and I'm pretty sure Bill knew from the beginning. You keep forgetting I was probably her only friend. I took her out for drinks the night her divorce went final. She got pretty well greased and told me how lucky I was to come from good people and that she'd cut all ties to what she called her former life. After a few more drinks, she said she was still in love with her ex. I told her she should go back and fight for him if that was how she really felt."

"Of course, *you* would say that," There was subtext behind the way Miss No Name stressed the word you, but I didn't have enough of the story to understand what that might be.

"So when it looked like she packed up and left," Carlene continued, "I thought she decided to fight for her man. I was happy for her but still peeved she hadn't bothered to say goodbye. I mean, how hard is it to tap a button on a cell phone? So you can see why I say Bill had no reason to kill her."

"I guess not, but wasn't he planning to break up

with her after the banquet? Maybe she didn't pack up to leave. Maybe he told her he'd hooked up with you, and they fought. Things got out of hand, and she ended up dead. He freaked out, packed up her stuff, so it only looked like she took off. Unless he was with you that night."

"Don't you think I'd know if I was sleeping with a murderer?"

I could attest to the fact that you could be married to a philanderer without knowing, so why would dating a murderer be such a stretch?

"I know Bill didn't kill anyone, and that's the end of this conversation," Carlene snarled.

Oh no, Carlene, I thought, that's only the beginning. It wasn't lost on me that Carlene hadn't alibied him for the night in question, which meant Bill had motive, means, and opportunity.

He had to be the killer. Who else could it be? The ex-husband? I didn't have enough information to know anything about him or their relationship, but on general principle, I couldn't come up with a strong motive. They were already divorced, so bumping her off for the insurance money wasn't a thing. Not reporting her missing was a point against him, but would he if they parted on bad terms? He might not have known she was gone. Probably not.

As much as I hated to do it, I bumped Carlene down to the bottom of my short list of suspects, where she tied for last place with Maryann. If I added the ex-husband, that still only left him and Bill at the top. It was time to talk to Bill.

# CHAPTER TWENTY-THREE

"You're late." Harley accused when I strolled up to where the men worked. Then he grinned. "But at least you sent a replacement. Better than Able did when Bill decided he was too good to show up on time."

In my head, I said a string of nasty words. Out loud, I said, "Bill's not coming today?" Suspicious timing if you asked me. Nobody did.

"He's running late," Able growled. "And when he shows, one of you," he swung a meaty, pointed finger between David and me, "will have to leave. One helper per person. That's the rule."

"Don't mind me." I let go of Molly's leash so she could run free. "I'm just here to watch and play with my dog. She doesn't get to stretch her legs out in my yard, so I thought I'd bring her along." I brandished the warped tennis racket and ball I'd brought along for her amusement. "There's nothing in the rules about how many spectators are allowed, right?"

Able returned my cheerful lilt with a glower. If he could fault my logic, he chose digging over arguing semantics. Going back for Molly had been a stroke of genius, and I wasn't lying when I said she could use the extended running room.

While I hit the ball for her, I ran over everything I'd learned that morning and came back to the same conclusion every time. Only two men in Grace's life—that I knew of anyway—had a motive to kill her the way they did. Bare-hands strangling is an up-close and personal method, most likely not premeditated, probably a crime of passion. Bill or the elusive ex-husband had to be the killer, and I only had access to one of them.

He arrived a few minutes later, looking just as bored as he had every day so far. I wondered if he sensed my increased interest, maybe even felt the hot breath of my pursuit on the back of his neck.

I know, I know. I'd been reading too many crime novels. Still, for a cold—or even a hot—blooded killer, he seemed fairly relaxed.

"Hey, Bill." I walked down to meet him as he neared the rest of the men. "I found this near your car the other day." I pulled the earring out of my pocket and held it up to show him. Molly hadn't been the only thing I went back to get. "I thought it might have fallen out."

Now, I'm not entirely sure what I expected him to do at that point. Preferably break down and confess his sins in front of God and country...or at least in front of the Mooselick River Treasure Hunter's Association. That didn't happen.

All he did was frown and say, "It's cute, but I'm more of a clip-on kind of guy." He tugged on one lobe to show it wasn't pierced. Laughter broke out behind me. Boring guy made a joke. Hardy har har.

Time to try something else. I locked my gaze to his face and said, "I've been looking at a lot of old newspaper articles about Grace Belanger. This looks like one she was wearing the night she died. Are you sure it didn't fall out of your car?"

Hearing Grace's name drew a flicker of emotion out of the man, but not the shame or guilt I expected to see. Only a touch of sadness.

"I wish she'd been in my car that night. It probably would have saved her life." I'd have bet mine he was sincere.

All my hopes of a dramatic revelation fizzled.

"Okay, then." I shoved the earring back in my pocket, clipped Molly's leash back on, and announced to no one that if they needed me, I'd be taking the dog for a walk down the quarry trail. I looked back once to see Bill still standing there staring at his shoes, and Able watching him as if wanting to offer comfort but not knowing how. Then Able turned his head to glare at me. It only lasted a moment, but I felt the heat of his displeasure even from a distance.

That had not gone how I planned at all.

Once out of sight, I pulled out my phone and tapped Ernie's personal cell phone number.

"I don't think Bill Cavanaugh killed Grace after all," I said when he answered.

"I'll take it under advisement." Ernie's tone said he wouldn't, but he relented to a point and gave me more information. "We found fingerprints on her car. Unless we get lucky and they're on file here, it'll take some time to run them through our database. We checked into her ex-husband and his alibi held. He was halfway across the country the night she went missing."

Just like that, both my suspects had been ruled

out, and there went my chances of putting Delly to rest.

Well, unless Bill had me completely snowed, and speaking of Delly, where had he been the last two days? It wasn't like him to miss an opportunity to talk my ear off, but then wasn't that just like a ghost? Haunting you day and night until you wanted them, then poof. Gone like the wind.

As we passed by the yellow flags of crime scene tape around the spot where Grace's killer buried her all that time ago, Molly stopped to chase her own tail. I knew exactly how she felt because I'd been doing plenty of that myself.

Who killed Grace?

Was it Maryann? Did she have the strength to choke the life out of someone? Would she smile while she did? Possible, but unlikely.

Was it Carlene? She could muster up the angry passion—that much anyone could see within two minutes of having to deal with her—but my gut insisted she was more bluff than bluster. If she meant to cut a person, she'd do it with her tongue and not a knife.

Was it Bill? He didn't seem the type to get riled up to the height of the kind of passion it would take to kill unless his perpetually bored demeanor covered up for a spark of personality he hadn't shown to me.

Or could it be some combination of people? Or someone else I hadn't even thought of yet? Several people in town could have wanted revenge, so really, it could have been anyone.

Well, hello, square one, it sucks to see you again.

Those were the thoughts running through my head as we came out along the bluff at the spot where Drew first noticed the flutter of plastic the day we found Grace. I'd been too preoccupied to notice my surroundings until I heard Delly's voice coming from somewhere close.

"Don't you cry now. Everything will come right in the end. You'll see. I'll stay right here with you. If I'd have known who you was before, I'd have tried to help when it mattered. I feel kind of bad about that now."

There was a pause, then Delly spoke again. "Somebody I know once said guilty consciences spark just as many good deeds as shining hearts. I suppose that's true enough, but I suppose you'll just have to take my intentions for what they're worth. We both been cheated out of what life had to offer, so maybe if we face the next one together, it won't be so hard."

When I heard Ernie's words repeated, and then the word cheated right after, it was as if someone turned on a light and rang a bell in my head at the same time. I knew who killed Grace and Delly. And I knew why.

His motive was iffy, at least as far as I was concerned, but I'd only run up against one man so concerned about cheating he'd practically delivered a sermon on the subject, and wouldn't a guilty conscience send such a man out to put his back into a job he thought utter folly? Grace would definitely fall into the cheater category, and for more reasons than one. The person I had in mind had a personal connection to her boyfriend, and people have been known to kill for the sake of protecting someone they loved. Everything fit—not like a glove or anything—but well enough my intuition was doing the found-the-killer dance.

I turned to go back the way I had come, then thought better of it. Delly deserved to hear the truth first.

"Molly, go find David." I gave a tug on the leash to pull her attention away from sniffing a spot in the grass, unclipped her, and watched her take off back up the trail. When she was out of sight, I hurried forward, reaching into my pocket for my phone as I went. First, I'd explain to Delly, then Ernie.

Around the next corner, I caught sight of the ghost who'd been haunting me and the one who hadn't. Grace Belanger was Delly's lady in red, and why hadn't I tripped to that before? She hovered next to him as he offered comfort.

"Hey, I—" was as far as I got before a killer stepped into view. "Hello, Able."

"You should have minded your own business and let the past stay dead."

"And you shouldn't have killed one of your closest friends." My fingers scrambled to pull my phone out of my pocket. I needed to call for help because the look on Able's face spelled murder, and this time it was my life on the line. "How could you? How could you hurt Delly like that? He never did a lick of harm to anyone. You said so yourself. Never cheated anyone out of so much as a nickel." I threw his own words back at him.

"I feel awful bad about how all that happened, and I'll feel bad when I have to watch your daddy mourn for you, but I can't see any way out of it now."

Looking past Able, I saw Delly's shocked face but knew I was on my own. Other ghosts might be able to channel anger into energy, but Delly just wasn't that kind of guy.

Worse, as I looked around a bit more, I realized Able had me cornered. The trail I'd followed to find the ghosts ran into a dead end with one side a cliff wall and the other a steep drop. The only way out was to go back, and Able had cut me off.

All I could do was keep him talking and hope someone came looking for me.

"What did Grace ever do to you?" At least if I died, I'd die knowing why.

"Told you before, I can't abide a cheater, and that girl was a cheater through and through. I was there when Martha took the call. Found out that girl had been sneaking around, making dirty deals in back rooms, and then there was what she done to Bill. She was bad news. I knew what I was supposed to do when I came up on her that night, sitting on the side of the road with a flat tire."

"So, it was like fate?"

Able pulled off his hat, used it to wipe the sweat off his neck, then put it back on, tugging the brim down low.

"It was." His hands fisted at his sides. "If she'd have shown a shred of remorse, I would have just helped her get back on the road, maybe talked to her a little bit about changing her ways. But I could see she was running. Suitcases in the backseat. She was running all right."

"Running where?"

"He's gone plumb crazy," Delly echoed my thoughts.

"Somewhere, I don't know, but I couldn't let her go knowing what she was, now could I?" He shook his head and took a step closer to me. I took one back.

And then another.

"And I can't let you go telling people what I done. I might not have been able to protect this town or poor Bill this time, but I know what to look for now. I won't let anything like that happen again."

He took another step. So did I. One more, and I'd be too close to the edge to have any chance at making it out of this alive.

Able was beyond reasoning. No one was coming to save me. My heart pounded, adrenaline flooded my body, and I heard Drew's voice in my head, saying things during that first self-defense class.

*Tell your attacker no, and make it loud.*

*Grab him by the shoulders and pull down.*

*Bring your knee up to make contact with his midsection.*

Okay, I could do all of that, but first, I had to know. "Why kill Delly? You got away with murder. Why did someone else have to die?"

"I said I was sorry how it happened, but I never killed Delly. I never would."

"He's right." Grace finally spoke. "I killed Delly."

"I don't understand," I said to both of them.

"I'd already done what I had to do when I come up on Delly near the edge of the quarry. I don't know how he knew. He must have seen the guilt on me, but I was ten, maybe fifteen feet away when he yelled out and run right off the cliff." Able's voice broke. "I tried to grab him, but there was nothing I could do. He was just gone."

"I told you I wasn't murdered, and as a general rule, I'm not scared of ghosts, but Grace here, she popped right up sudden-like, and yelled out. Jumped me, and I lost my balance."

Able's face hardened, but his eyes burned with madness. "I'll tell the same story about you."

This time when he stepped toward me, I met him halfway.

"No," I shouted in his face. Everything seemed to

slow down for a moment, so I got to enjoy Able's shocked expression right before I yanked down on his shoulders and aimed my knee just below his ribcage. My body took over after that, and I followed through with a downward slice of the back of my fist that took him right at the bridge of his nose.

Able went down, but on the way, managed to give me a hard shove that sent me careening toward the edge of the cliff and that weightless moment right before a fall. With too much momentum, I couldn't stop myself, and I knew I was done. I could see the end coming closer, and then a chocolate blur shot in from out of nowhere. Molly circled around me at breakneck speed, slammed her body into mine, and yelped when we made contact. We went down in a tangle of bodies, landing far too close to the precipice.

Close enough we dislodged a flurry of small stones and a shower of dirt that slipped over the edge. Behind me, I heard Able struggle to his feet, his footsteps lumbering closer. Molly had saved me, but it would be too little, too late.

On the plus side, if I was dead, I wouldn't have to testify at Paul's hearing.

"Able Gallow, stop right there, and put your

hands on your head." Ernie's voice rang out behind me. I twisted to see him coming down the path, gun raised and pointed at Able's head. Able had left his fingerprints on Grace's car. Ernie knew where to find him, and in a twist of luck arrived just in time.

"Stop, or I'll shoot."

Yes, cops really do fall back on the clichés sometimes.

# CHAPTER TWENTY-FOUR

"Don't rush me," I held my phone up at roughly eye level, looked at the photo of the sketch, and then at the house to get my bearings. What was left of the Mooselick Treasure Hunters Association waited patiently enough, considering they all thought the chances of finding Clint's gold were less than nil.

"This is where the garden would have been. I think the bench sat right about here with the hydrangea behind it." I could all but feel eyes rolling behind me, but they'd had their chance to choose where to search, and now it was mine. I moved to the spot where I thought the tree had been and spun slowly in place to see if I could suss out the most likely direction to take.

"The barn was just over there." I pointed and swung what I considered was enough distance to sight a path that would have been clear back in the days when Clint hid his gold. "That way."

I walked toward the maple tree where we'd begun our search the first day, counting my paces as I went. A hundred and fifty took me within a few steps of the massive trunk. Without saying another word, I thumbed the metal detector switch to the on position, though by then, I didn't need it to tell me this was the spot. I just knew.

But the men needed to hear it, so I waved what passed for a magic wand over the ground and let out a whoop when I heard the deep-throated beep.

"This is it, boys. Get out your shovels."

Delly watched the first jar come up out of the ground, his eyes shining, a grin on his face to rival a kid on Christmas morning.

"I told you it was there. Didn't I tell you?"

Because we weren't alone, I merely nodded, but he didn't take my nonverbal reply as a lack of enthusiasm.

"It's heavy," Dad weighed the jar in one hand, then used the other to brush away some of the soil from the rim. "Here's the true test, though." The sound of metal and dirt crunching against glass made me cringe as though it were nails on a chalkboard as he grunted with effort.

The lid didn't so much pop off as disintegrate, but

the results were the same. Upending the jar, he pulled out a single gold nugget, which could be measured against the tip of his thumb.

Metal tinged against glass. "I've got one over here," Harley let Junior do the honor of drawing the jar from its dark home. They didn't bother wrestling with the lid, only wiped away enough dirt to see the contents.

"This one's light. Looks like mostly flake."

Most of the oohing and ahhing had stopped by the time the third jar came to light with David grinning above the shovel. "This one's heavy." He set it aside, moving on to dig at the base of the next flag.

"Show me." Naked longing twisted Delly's face into a less affable version as at least a dozen lumps fell into my palm, their surfaces knobby and without glitter. Ghosts don't breathe, but they often forget the habits of a lifetime, and so Delly went through the motion without actually inhaling.

"That's Clint's folly, and I suppose mine as well. He died in a storm while keeping everything back for a rainy day, and I spent too much time chasing rainbows."

I tried to convey my sympathy with only a look, but as in life, so in death, you can't keep a good man down. "But I guess it's no folly to catch a killer. I'll tell your grandmother all about it if I run into her in the afterlife."

As he walked into the light, Delly dropped a final bomb. "Tell your friend at the inn not to pay no nevermind to Ned Sanders. He's a cranky one, even for a ghost."

*When Everly agreed to be Patrea's maid of honor, she thought she'd be wearing a dress to the wedding—not her sleuthing Hat.*

Keep reading for a preview of the next book, Wedding Ghost, where it's up to Everly to avenge another ghost before Patrea says, "I do."

~Also Available in Audiobook & Paperback Versions~

## Quick Author's Note

Hi there! We're ReGina and Erin—mother, daughter,

and the ones who try to keep Everly Dupree out of too much trouble (and usually fail).

Thank you for joining us on another of Everly's ghostly adventures! This time around, her search for answers got tangled up in rumors of hidden treasure—and as Everly learned, the only thing more stubborn than a small-town legend is the ghost who refuses to let it go.

Next up is Wedding Ghost, where Everly's best friend Jacy is planning her big day... but with Everly's luck, there's bound to be a little something borrowed, a little something blue, and probably a ghost or two.

Anyway, if you've come this far with us and not decided we're complete and total whackadoodles... and especially if you have, we're offering a chance to sign up for our newsletters— the best place to get new release updates, sales notifications, and other fun content.

You can sign up for ReGina's newsletter and/or Erin's newsletter and as a thank-you gift for hanging out with us, you'll also get a FREE novella that isn't available anywhere else. And of course, we promise not to SPAM your inbox!

Love, hugs, and happy reading,
*ReGina & Erin*

P. S. If you enjoyed this book, it would be great if you could leave a review or recommendation on Amazon, GoodReads or BookBub.

Your reviews help indie authors sell more books!

"That's weird." On Saturday, Patrea knocked on the door of Merry Eats for the third time, then cupped her eyes with her palms, pressing the sides of her hands against the window to block out enough light for a decent look through the textured glass. "I don't smell anything cooking, and I don't hear anyone moving around in there. She wouldn't flake on me again, right?"

She tried the door, and it opened. We exchanged a look before stepping over the threshold. The familiar sinking sensation in my stomach and the dead silence boded ill.

Patrea beat me to the door, took one look, and backed away. I already had my phone in my hand when I walked past her. "We're too late," I said, needlessly. Face gray, eyes wide and staring, her head lying in a pool of vomit—that Summer was gone was painfully obvious. That her death hadn't been an easy one, even more so. A wave of sympathy over-whelmed me—what a sad waste of a life.

Carol Ann Wilmette answered the emergency call. Why was she always on duty whenever I found a dead body? And yes, I am aware that the larger question should have been, why was I *always* finding corpses, but at this point, I'd decided to stop asking that one.

"911, what's your emergency?" Carol Ann asked again.

"Uh, it's Everly Dupree."

"Who's dead now?"

"Why do you assume someone's dead every time I call?"

I heard the pop of a gum bubble. "So someone's not dead? What's your emergency, then?"

I sighed. "No, someone is."

There was an expectant silence on the other end of the phone, then the bubble sound again. "You gonna tell me, or do I have to guess?"

"It's Summer Merryfield. You'd better send Ernie over to the café right away."

"You want me to stay on the line until he gets there?"

Carol must have had some new training because

she'd never asked me that before. "No, I know the drill. Don't touch anything, don't move the body. Just send him over." I tapped the end button and put my phone away.

Patrea lurched toward the small table near the door, put her hands down on it to steady herself, then pulled out one of the chairs and sat. She looked at me much the same as I suspected Carol would have if I'd walked into the station. I don't mind saying it hurt a little.

"I didn't do anything," I defended myself. "Don't look at me like I'm the harbinger of death. It's not my fault if I keep ending up in the wrong place at the wrong time."

"How awful is it that my first thought was there goes the food for my wedding?" Patrea pressed two fingers in the spot between her eyebrows. "I'm a self-ish, horrible person."

Taking care to stay back from the body, I reassured Patrea while trying to take in as many details as possible just in case Summer's death hadn't been accidental.

"Of course, you're not. We all have those weird reflex thoughts when confronted with death. It's only natural." I skirted the steel-topped table where

Summer had been working, made my way to the stove, grabbed a set of tongs from a nearby container, and used them to lift the lid of a pot and look at its cold, congealed contents.

"You're not supposed to touch anything, remember?" Patrea's voice sounded tired.

"I didn't touch the stove." My voice sounded defensive.

"You touched the tongs."

So I had, I thought, dismayed. And since it was too late to go back and undo what I had done, I used them to open one of the oven doors letting out a waft of the scent of something sweet. The smell came from a baking sheet containing a single layer of pale, green stalks sliced at an angle that made them look like a bit like pasta and coated in sugar that looked to have gone damp and sticky.

The second oven held a pan of herb-studded chicken that looked about half cooked. I nudged the door shut with my knee. Both ovens had been turned off before the food had time to finish cooking.

"I'll fess up when Ernie gets here. And you touched the chair and the table." I didn't tack on a *so there*, but my tone did.

I circled the body looking for signs of foul play

but saw nothing obvious. Summer lay on her side, her body curved inward. I couldn't see or smell blood, but that could have been masked by the smell of vomit.

"Looks like Summer ate something that disagreed with her."

With no telltale chill in the air, no chatty ghost hovering, either, I assumed we hadn't disturbed an active crime scene and said as much to Patrea.

"I'll be the judge of that," Ernie hadn't made any noise as he entered the café, probably because we'd left the door open behind us. "What did you touch, Everly?"

As succinctly as possible, I told Ernie what I'd done. As he knelt to examine Summer's body, I explained how we'd come to find her lying on her kitchen floor. Patrea pitched in to back me up. The story didn't take long to tell, and by the time it was done, the ambulance had pulled up out front.

"That's it," I said. "I met the woman for the first time yesterday, and now she's gone. It's sad, really." I stepped back to let the medics bring in their equipment, recognizing the first man through the door.

Vinnie De Luca was here in both his current positions. I suspected he'd been elected to be the county's coroner because he had at least some medical train-ing, and no one else wanted the job. Maybe if we lived in a larger area, the poor man could have given up his paramedic shifts and spent his days just wearing one hat...or would that be one lab coat? I'd heard through the grapevine—in the form of Martha Tipton—that Vinnie had applied to work for the state medical examiner in some capacity. According to Martha, Vinnie had aspirations—she'd wrinkled her nose over the word—that involved moving to Augusta.

"Poison," he said after a quick examination. "Would be my first guess. Accidental, most likely. We'll have to send her to Augusta for an autopsy. The lab techs will have to run a tox screen to be certain." He stood and scanned the items scattered across the tall, steel-topped table where Summer had been slicing and dicing ingredients. "It'll take time for the results to come back."

"Any way you can get the ME to put a rush on it?" Ernie said.

"I've got some pull, but probably not enough to move us to the front of the line for what's clearly death by misadventure. I'll do what I can, though."

While he talked, Vinnie picked up samples of the

chopped vegetables, dropped them in small plastic bags, and set them aside. He did the same with the contents of a lidless, plastic container that looked like the one we'd seen with the sorbet. Next, he went over to the stockpot, sniffed the contents, then took a small sample of that and another from the contents of the tray in the oven.

Part of Vinnie's job was to look at the evidence and decide the cause of death, but that pronouncement generally came after the autopsy. If Ernie suspected homicide, he could call the state police and a tech team to investigate the crime. Since he was on the spot, and because he leaned toward an accidental poisoning, it looked like Vinnie had decided to take on the job all by himself.

"Shouldn't you call in someone more official to do that?"

Ernie glared at me when I asked, but Vinnie answered before Ernie had a chance to tell me to mind my business.

"I'm this close," he held up his thumb and index finger with less than half an inch between them, "to finishing my degree in forensics. I think I'm capable of collecting evidence," he said in a how-dare-you-question-me tone.

A tall, square trash can lined with a black plastic bag sat at the end of Summer's worktable. As Vinnie passed by the can, he glanced down, then stopped short, and looked harder. Whatever he saw there sent his eyebrows upward and had him reaching into one of his pockets for a pair of rubber gloves, which he put on with practiced movements.

"Find something?" Ernie's shoes squeaked on the tile as he walked over to take a look for himself. He reached down, possibly to tilt the can toward better lighting, but Vinnie swatted Ernie's hand away before it made contact.

"Don't touch that with your bare hands, you fool."

Ernie's face flushed a dull red at being called a fool, but he kept his cool. Another reason why I maintain Ernie is a good cop.

"That's Cicuta maculata. Commonly known as water hemlock. Every part of the plant is poisonous. We'll need to send a sample to the lab to be certain, but this is gonna be your cause of death. I'll stake my reputation and stand you a week's pay if I'm wrong."

Too cool to flinch, Ernie slowly and deliberately shoved his hand in his pocket, rocked up on his toes to get a look at the offending plant matter. "You sure? Looks like Queen Anne's lace from here."

"I'm sure. The diameter of the stems is a dead giveaway."

Vinnie's poor choice of term earned him a sidelong look from Patrea, but by unspoken agreement, we'd stayed quiet during the past few minutes. Call me nosy, but I didn't want Ernie kicking us out until we'd heard everything there was to hear.

"Something like this happens every year or two in Maine. You get your amateur botanists who insist on foraging for mushrooms and other edibles, and they're never careful enough. Mistake destroying angel mushrooms for white caps or hemlock for angelica, and instead of a nicely seasoned meal, they're serving up a plateful of death."

I heard Patrea suck in a breath at about the same time I realized that, had Summer not taste-tested her own dish, we'd have been tucking into that plateful of death right about now. All the blood drained out of my face leaving it, I was sure, paler than it naturally was, which was saying something. Intense emotions washed over me—fear, relief, sorrow—leaving a chill in their wake. I shivered. Beside me, Patrea did the same and clasped her hands together to stop them from shaking.

It wasn't my first brush with death, but this time things were different. The danger hadn't come at me from the front in an all-out assault but sneaked up from behind. This time, I didn't have any sort of adrenaline rush to carry me along, so the impact hit harder.

"I suppose she's better off this way." Ernie watched the paramedics put on extra protection before attending to the body. "If she'd have opened up for lunch, no telling how many people she'd have killed."

"The hell I would." Summer's voice came from behind me and turned my veins to icy streams. I closed my eyes slowly and hoped that when I opened them again, it would be to wake up from a bad dream.

A doomed wish, of course.

"Condescending jackass. Who does he think he is?" Summer ranted. "My grandmother taught me more than he'll ever know about wild edibles. I'm not some idiot wandering the woods with a guidebook and no clue. I have eyes, don't I? And a nose. And more than half a brain, too."

With every syllable she uttered, Summer's ear-popping energy rose higher. I felt the prickle across the back of my neck, the buzzing in my throat, the tiny hairs standing up along my arms. Surrounded by people who clearly weren't able to sense the disturbance—though I did see a shudder run through Patrea's body, and she had once mentioned feeling a presence in my house—I couldn't turn and tell Summer to shut up. I dearly wanted to, mind you, but not as much as I wanted to avoid giving Ernie one more reason to look at me funny. So, I kept quiet and let her run down.

"I've been cooking with angelica for years. I've never poisoned anyone before, and I certainly wouldn't be stupid enough to cut up hemlock with my bare hands. Do you see any gloves laying around here, genius?"

Summer waved her finger under the ME's nose. "Do you? And look at my hands. Are there contact burns on them? No, there are not, and there would be if I were stupid enough to handle hemlock without protection. How did you get that job anyway?"

Vinnie didn't even flinch when she put her face close to his. I did, though. Maybe other people can't feel anything, but being that close to a ghost isn't a pleasant experience for me. The nearest real-life experience I can compare it to is walking barefooted through ankle-deep muck. Touching a ghost is like that, only over my entire body, and the muck is icy cold besides.

The thing that finally shut Summer up was the sound of the zipper closing on the body bag. Maybe she hadn't fully realized she was dead until then, but she quit talking right in the middle of a sentence and seemed to become more aware of her surroundings. I watched from the sidelines hoping she wouldn't notice I could see her.

Would I feel lousy if she didn't know there was someone in the living world who might help her find justice should there come the need? Probably, but I figured I could live with the guilt if it meant her not following me home and bugging me until I did.

Mooselick River is the kind of small town where people will follow an ambulance or fire truck out of morbid curiosity. Plus, Carol Ann Wilmette has a big mouth. Whether she called Summer's ex, or some other lookie-loo did, the result was the same because he picked that moment to show up and shove his way past the pair of deputies Ernie had called in to help.

"Summer?" Jack Merryfield stumbled to a halt at

the sight of the black body bag being loaded onto a gurney for transport. "It can't be." Frantic, he searched the room for someone who might tell him what had happened. When his gaze fell on Patrea and me, he frowned, then latched onto Ernie as the best possible source of information.

"What happened? I heard...tell me that's not Summer." He moved closer to the gurney, and I think he would have gone for the zipper if Ernie hadn't stepped in front of him.

"Don't!" Given in a gentler tone than I'd have expected, the command still stopped Jack from following through on his quest for assurance that Summer was dead. "Let Vinnie take care of her now."

"I don't understand." Breathing heavy, Jack grabbed the front of Ernie's shirt. "Tell me what happened."

For an ex-husband, the man took distraught to a new level. Watching him melt down put my response to the situation into perspective, calmed my anxiety a notch or two. Patrea's, too, I guessed when I caught her expression.

And then, I made my fatal mistake. I looked over at Summer to see what she might be thinking, and she caught me. Her eyes widened as she hovered nearby.

"You can see me."

Too late, I tried to let my gaze pass over her as if she weren't there, but it wasn't enough.

"You can see me." She said again with such relief I couldn't help myself. I looked at her deliberately, nodded my head slowly, then tried to communicate using subtle expressions that we couldn't talk with everyone around.

I wasn't looking forward to the moment when she got me alone because, in my experience, her presence could only mean one thing: murder.

Wedding Ghost is available now. Keep reading for a preview of the free novella you'll get for joining our newsletters.

# Excerpt from A Snowball's Chance in Spell

~

Lightning flirted in shadows of the dark clouds hovering over my house when I came home from work the afternoon before my twenty-second Christmas Eve. Nothing unusual there. With three elemental faeries living in the house, weird weather happened all the time. Or rather, every time my temperamental godmothers mounted some sort of snit.

The godmothers idled at snit.

Going back to work wasn't an option. I'd cleared the last match of the year—a lovely couple with a shared affection for online gaming—and I was no coward. When it came to diffusing faerie fights, I consider myself an expert, and this one didn't look like it rated more than a two on the volcano scale.

Yes, you heard right. I measure faerie fights on the scale of whether or not a volcano might erupt in my backyard. Living with faeries is never boring. Occasionally dangerous—especially because I have yet to come into the magic that is my birthright, but never boring.

A quick check proved they'd contained the madness to the inside and/or the backyard. The two feet of snow on the front lawn was still there and still white—you try explaining black snow to your neighbors sometime. I didn't see any winged denizens—fae or otherwise—dotting the roof ridge, or hear any ominous sounds. If not for the fact that lightning is rare in Maine during the winter, and rarer still when confined to a single area, I'd have thought it was a quiet day in the household.

In my head, I downgraded the threat to a level one, and went inside.

For the most part, my place looks like an ordinary, New England style home. Built by my great grandparents, it's the oldest house in a neighborhood that grew up around it when the suburbs expanded into what was once a rural area. Because, I think, the faeries wanted to give me a normal upbringing, they left the house in mostly the same condition it was in when they came to take care of me and only added on a wing for their own use.

I stepped into the front hall expecting...well, just about anything. Did I mention the faeries love holidays? Maybe they don't have them in the faelands, or maybe they do and go overboard there, too. I can't say since I've never been, but I could tell at a glance there were more decorations than there had been when I left.

"Terra!" I yelled, but got no answer. Terra, faerie of earth, held sway over all the flora and fauna found on dry land. She would be the one responsible for the pine boughs twining over anything that held still long enough. Fire faerie, Soleil, contributed by setting sparks of faerie light to twinkle inside the delicate ice bubbles crafted by her sister, Evian, mistress of water. The effect was lovely, but not as lovely as the three women could be when their faces weren't twisted, as they were now, with rage.

I came upon them in their favorite fighting grounds: the kitchen. It looked like I'd caught this one early since there was relatively little damage done so far. Steam rose from a puddle of water at Soleil's feet which I assumed had come from Evian. Vines snaked from between the kitchen tiles to twine around Evian's ankles, and there were a few smoking embers dotting Terra's hair. Nothing more than a minor spat.

Keeping it casual, I asked, "What's going on?"

There's no rhyme or reason to what will settle a fight or send one into the red zone.

Terra turned one granite pink eye in my direction. "This doesn't concern you." The fingers of her left hand twitched and the vines slithered from Evian's ankles to her knees.

Retaliating, Evian conjured a gush of water from thin air, and doused the smoking embers. The scent of pine boughs couldn't compete with the stench of burnt hair, or the pungent funk erupting from the flowers that burst into bloom near her feet.

"Now look," I pointed out to Terra before she conjured something worse. "Evian is trying to help."

"Was not." Evian snapped her fingers and turned Terra's wet hair white with frost, except because the vines were now questing higher, she overshot the mark and doused a few of Soleil's decorative sparkles.

That was the moment I lost control.

Oh, who am I kidding? I never had control.

Soleil let out a screech and lobbed a fireball at Evian, who encased it in a ball of water and batted it toward Terra. I felt scoured clean when Terra called all the dirt and dust in the house to form a layer over the bobbing ball of doom which now resembled a small planet whizzing back toward Soleil.

It might have ended better if I'd have kept my mouth shut, but I didn't.

"You're going to put an eye out with that thing."

The ire of three faeries is a potent thing, but not as potent as a flaming mudball. I ducked, rolled, and hit the latch on the patio door in what I'd like to think was a graceful move. Probably looked like a seal rolling off a rock.

The flaming fireball arced over my head, its warm breeze tossing my hair, and rocketed off into the sky.

Crisis averted. Except, it wasn't. I should have known.

**A Snowball's Chance in Spell** is only available by signing up for one of our newsletters here:
https://reginawelling.com
https://erinlynnwrites.com

If you'd like to meet more people who live rent-free in our heads, here's a list of other series we've written. Our books are all set in fictional towns in Maine, and some characters like to flit back and forth between series. The cast of Psychic Seasons hangs out with Everly and also with Lexi Balefire from the Fate Weaver series. Mag and Clara Balefire are Lexi's grandmother and aunt!

*Psychic Seasons*
Four women, four love stories, and a whole lot of supernatural surprises. In the quaint town of Oakville, Maine, psychic visions, ghostly whispers, and fate itself conspire to change lives—and hearts—forever

*Haunted Everly After*
Everly Dupree came home for a fresh start—not a full-time gig solving ghostly murders. But when the

dearly departed start demanding justice, what's a reluctant medium to do?

*Ponderosa Pines Mysteries*
Nothing bad ever happens in the weird little town of Ponderosa Pines...until someone dies. Now it's up to best friends Chloe and EV to solve the mystery—before the town's secrets bury them too.

*Fate Weaver*
Lexi Balefire—matchmaker, witch, and accidental fate-weaver—must balance love, magic, and a family legacy of chaos before destiny decides for her!

*Mag and Clara Balefire Mysteries*
Sister witches Mag and Clara Balefire move to a sleepy Maine town for a fresh start—only to find themselves conjuring up trouble, solving murders, and keeping their magic under wraps in this charmingly witchy cozy mystery series

*Laurel Haven Witches*
Four witches, destined by blood and magic, must embrace their power, battle a dark legacy, and

surrender to the love that could break the curse—or bind them to it forever.

*Nell Page: Accidental Investigator*

Nell Page owns a bookstore, drinks too much coffee, and has a habit of noticing things she probably shouldn't. With warmth, wit, and an accidental talent for investigating, Nell tackles mysteries that don't always involve murder—but always matter.